SONG OF BLOOD AND ASHES
a Vampire tale

by

GERALD BRENNAN

෨෬

DREAMSTREET PRESS
ANN ARBOR, MI USA
www.DreamStreetPress.com

ISBN-13: 978-1-7350802-0-8

to

Buddy & June

Song of Blood and Ashes

a Vampire tale

༺ འ ༻

1

Aidan feels uncomfortable on the new bike ever since he bought it in New York.

In Ireland he briefly rode a Harley Davidson Dyna, but it was ten years-old, well broken-in by the fellow from whom Aidan Bell had seized it. This new bike is a BWM R18, with a seat for two. (Ladies do thrill at a ride with him.) It feels stiff, though it is superior in almost every aspect to that decade-old Harley-Davidson back home, a little heavier maybe, but he will get used to it.

At the moment he feels self-conscious, as if price tags were hanging off of the bike and people were sniggering at him. He's still not accustomed to the new riding position, and his shins get a little warm so close to the engine. The stiff new jeans and new leathers add to his discomfort. And this is *so* not Dublin. He is a stranger in a strange land. But well-equipped, and wealthy.

His wanderings from his old world have taken him to the Midwest of the United States of America. He took I-80 straight through to the Toledo area, riding by night, and decided to head north through Michigan, ending up on US-23. He exited on the M-14 freeway in Ann Arbor, and decided to check out the little town. As a music student on a career path in Dublin, he knew Ann Arbor's reputation as a scholarly center.

Headed now south down Main Street, Aidan putters through downtown and stops at the light on Liberty Street, mid-town, where two couples sit at a table enjoying coffee drinks in the cool night air. The girls are co-ed cute and the boys look street-wise and smart-assed. They stare at him, the girls with interest and the boys with contempt; he wishes the light would change.

"Fuck any hogs lately?" one of the boys calls out to him. Aidan gives him a blank look. The boy has a mess of acne and a shaved head. *How do assholes like this end up with such beautiful girls?* The boy across from him looks embarrassed and whispers something to Pimples, who shakes his head and laughs.

"Got that big bike 'cause your wiener is so small?" he yells at Aidan, who muscles his bike to the curb and removes his helmet. The girls swoon subtly, and the boys stiffen a bit in their chairs. Aidan fixes his eyes on Pimples' girl and smiles. She smiles back.

Now, Aidan is of two minds. One says, primally, beat the bejesus out of Pimples and slake his thirst with him; his other mind reminds him that the stupid lad hasn't done anything to quite merit such a response, though he has 'thug' written all over him. Aidan considered how humiliation might also work nicely here.

"What's your name, darlin'?" Aidan calls over the idle throb of the big bike to Pimples' significant other.

"None o' your business!" Pimples calls back. But she keeps looking at Aidan and smiling back.

"Andrea."

"Well, Andrea darlin'," he says in a heavy brogue that charms her from hair to hoof, "hop on and we'll go for a ride, you and me."

It is more of an order than a question, and her girlfriend elbows her and whispers something in her ear.

"Hey!" Pimples grabs the sides of the table and threatens to rise from his plastic chair, offended. Andrea and Aidan ignore the display. Pimples points down the road. "Keep goin', asshole!"

"Where will we go?" Andrea asks Aidan.

"We're goin' wherever you want to go," and he holds out his gloved hand, pulling it back, removing the glove, and re-offers his bare hand to the girl. Andrea pushes out her chair and rises.

"Where the fuck you think you're going?" Pimples inquires loudly, bolting upright on his plastic chair which topples and clatters behind him.

Andrea steps to the curb and takes Aidan's hand. "Wherever I *want* to go," she calls back, "like he says." She holds onto his hand and a frown creases her brow. "God," she looks up at Aidan. "Your hands are cold!"

Aidan ignores that and scoots forward a bit, while Andrea, in her yellow shorts and skinny yellow top, artlessly but charmingly squirms in behind Aidan and puts her arms around his chest. Aidan replaces his glove and helmet casually, eyeing Pimples with a smile.

"Don't come back, bitch!" Pimples threatens in a roaring voice. Andrea flips him the bird and the pair are off down Main Street in a loud rumble. Andrea is thrilled, clutching tightly to Aidan as they head out of downtown, passing homes and sidewalks teeming with lots of people, young and old, enjoying the evening.

They soon come upon the biggest stadium that Aidan has ever seen, and he is so captivated by it that a pickup truck behind him has to honk twice before Aidan wakes up and heeds the green light in front of him.

They come directly upon a large school and Aidan rumbles into the parking lot, then stops abruptly. Andrea tilts in her seat and leans forward to get Aidan's attention. "So? You haven't asked me where I want to go," she reminds him in a seductive voice.

Aidan never even makes eye-contact. "I don't care a rat's arse where you want to go," he tells her flatly. "Get off."

"What?" she startles. "But we never—"

"There's no *we*," he harshes.

She twists free of her perch and stands to face him. "You know, I thought you were... you're an *asshole!*" she shouts. "At least give me a ride back to-" but the rest is lost to Aidan as he spins the Beemer round in a cloud of dust, spraying the indignant girl with pebbles and dirt, and back to Main Street, heading south, out of town.

After a few minutes of cruising, over the freeway and into the countryside, it occurs to Aidan, sunset long past and the world winding down, that Ann Arbor is as good a place as any to start being an American, in many ways better than most. It is clean, cultured in its small way, big enough not to bore, full of beautiful women, and small enough to know well and quickly. It will work, for now. He checks his mirrors and makes the U-turn back to town, and a nice room, maybe the Hilton, for the night.

But Aidan is getting hungry, and he hopes he isn't too late to make good on the obvious dinner choice.

He hurries the big bike back into town and parks behind the café where he had been insulted by Pimples. He removes his gloves, jacket and helmet, and stuffs them inside his saddle bag.

There is a rear entrance to the café, and he enters, not sure how to proceed. On the off chance of the encounter he seeks he notes the men's room sign and takes a peek inside. Now it seems to Aidan that Ann Arbor is doing its best to welcome him with open arms, for there at the urinal stands Pimples zipping up. He turns his head and spies Aidan.

"You!" he blurts.

Aidan smiles. "It's me! What of it?"

Pimples takes a step back and pulls a small knife from a belt sheath. Aidan breathes a happy sigh. Pimples springs upon Aidan with vicious slashes. "Where is-" and he would have no more words forever.

Aidan seizes the lad by the neck with his hand, stifling Pimples' would-be screams. Aidan sinks his suddenly elongated and razor-sharp canines precisely on target and feeds voluptuously until the violent thrashings of his quarry cease. The door could open any moment to a most unpleasant interruption, but the city's welcome continues even while Aidan, undisturbed, drags the corpse of his prey into the toilet stall and sits him, dead, upon the throne.

He closes the stall door and checks the bathroom mirror for blood on his person. Aidan is meticulous about this sort of thing and notes with pride that not a single red smudge can be detected on his newly ruddy and glowing visage. But he notes a serious case of helmet-hair that he fluffs out with his hands, and the door opens. A young, looks like a Korean fellow, enters, nodding to Aidan who returns the civility with a smile, and slips out the closing door. What good luck all around! It is clear that Ann Arbor wants him as much as he wants to call the city his new home.

In a jiffy he is back to his bike, re-jacketed and helmeted and ready to ride, but a bit unsteady. *Yes*, he affirms, *Ann Arbor seems like a swell little town*. As he has this merry thought, his gaze is upon a pretty young woman standing near. But he blinks and now there are two of her. Double-vision. He giggles, and thinks, *Wow, Pimples must have been smashed by the time I got to him*. Aidan was drunk on his meal, and there was something else mixed in that he could not identify. He giggles again and realizes he is too intoxicated to drive. But this has never stopped him before. He roars away, back to Main Street, then left on the town's main artery, called Huron Street, and decides to explore what lies west.

Aidan's motorcycle

Aidan drunkenly but politely pays cash in advance for three nights at a place called Weber's, away from downtown and central campus, which he thinks too congested. Three days he reckons will be enough time for him to find a decent house, which he will purchase, not rent. The last thing he needs to deal with is a landlord—always a crapshoot.

Sitting on the firm hotel couch with crossed arms, sobering slightly and staring into the vacant hole of the dormant TV, Aidan muses about his imminent requirements. 'Need' and 'want' are no longer functional ideas to him; 'requirements,' that is what he is all about now.

He *requires* a piano. *That* he will lease. Also, a sound system will need to be purchased. Also, a PC and a TV. Appliances will be purchased, mainly for their appearance. He has little need for refrigeration (although he likes his vodka ice-cold) nor for any cooking apparatus, but anyone who comes by will be suspicious of a gutted kitchen. "I don't cook much," just doesn't seem like it will cut it. He will need a bed and room darkening shades all around. Some bookcases will be required, and a most comfortable La-Z-Boy. Maybe two.

Aidan is exhausted. Instead of sleeping he *rode* the day away, but he is still too restless (and uncomfortably intoxicated) this evening to fall into that dark refuge. So, he decides to watch inane American late-night TV until he can't stand it anymore, which happens disappointingly quickly. Next he peruses the Arbor News, getting a feel for the local rag. Then, about 3 a.m., he decides to simply meditate until sunrise, when he will close the curtains and, at last, sleep.

He wakes, refreshed, and looks over at the clock on the desk. It reads 5:13 p.m., so, a good three hours before he can wander about the city *ad libitum*. He dresses (he always sleeps nude), sits on the one comfortable chair and reaches for his new phone. It's dead. *Shit!* He rises, and roots around his pack for the charging cord, plugs the phone in and turns it on.

He requires a computer and decides that, even once settled into his own home, a laptop is probably the way to go. He locates a Best Buy that is open late not too far from the motel, and he will head there tonight to make the purchase. He decides to while away a couple hours looking seriously at the local real estate, wishing he had the laptop right now instead of the tiny phone for such a duty.

Aiden is astonished at the prices of homes in Ann Arbor. It's not that he can't afford them, he is just plainly shocked at the prices. He scribbles a few addresses to look at (one in particular, available immediately) and decides to check them out with a drive-by after he buys his laptop.

He wants to be far from the University, somewhere on the outskirts of the city, somewhere with few neighbors and fewer students, quiet. He doesn't need much room, so the McMansions (of which plenty in the area) are out. Also old houses are of no interest—Aiden wants the spectre of upkeep and maintenance to rear its ugly head as rarely as possible.

It is now nearly 7 p.m. and Aiden is thirsty. Not for nourishment, but for alcohol. He moseys on downstairs to the bar and restaurant facility. Very nice. A jazz band is setting up and will play soon. Aiden isn't in the mood for that scene and requests a table far away.

There is no hint, looking at him sitting in the restaurant, that he is a deadly leather-clad hell-raiser with a scary big motorcycle; he looks like a young professor.

"A Stoli martini, straight-up, dry, with a twist," Aidan says to the middle-age, middle-height, middling pretty server.

"From Ireland? Are you?" This happens all the time now.

"Yes!" Aidan proclaims. "And this city shall be my new home."

"Well!" this gladdens her. "I hope we'll see you here often!" she bubbles. He senses her genuineness and gives her a grateful smile, and off she goes to get his martini. He perceives her innate goodness, and such as she will always be safe from such as he, though there is really no one else like him. He feeds exclusively on violence and evil.

When he was new, back in Dublin, he fed on anything human. There were no selection criteria; there was only a psychotic hunger that required slaking *now!* There was no judgement. There was no control. But this ecstatic condition did not last. Eventually his mind caught up with the blank reckless craving of his body and he was forced to confront his actions and their consequences. This distinguishes him from his few peers who cannot be bothered with these niceties of conscience. No one, save for his dam, understands what sets him apart.

Still, even now, when he looks back on his year of rampant hunger, and with the inconceivable carnage of those months finally jelled and clarified in his mind, he weeps bitter tears. How can he ever bring balance to those unforgivable deeds? Is there any compensation he can make?

"Here you go, sir." She is back with his drink, places it in front of him, and recoils a little at the sight of him. "Are you alright?"

Aiden wipes bloody tears from his cheek and manages a wan smile.

"Allergies," he claims.

"Oh. I see," she says, concerned. "I'll bring some extra napkins."

"Thank you," and he looks at her badge, "…Karen. But wait a bit." Aiden picks out the twist of lime, shoots his martini down in a single draught and hands her the glass. "And another one of these, please, if you would, love. And not so much vermouth."

Aidan has three more, signs for the drinks, tips extravagantly in cash (the tipping thing in America has been hard to sort out), and heads upstairs to dress for the evening.

Those who might have spotted him in the restaurant would never recognize him as the same man now as he descends the stair. He is clad with black leather from boots to gloved hands and jacketed neck. His face is visible because he's wearing his night helmet, which lacks a face shield. He exits the place and spies a couple of other bikers unlocking their Hondas as he approaches his BMW. They greet one another and one of the fellows makes an appreciative gesture toward Aiden's ride.

"Nice bike, man. Real sweet."

Aiden mounts his steed and nods appreciatively at the young man. "Thanks."

"Wouldn't figure you for the helmet, though."

Aiden is confused. "It's the law, no?"

"Hell no," the young man replies. "Not in Michigan. Not no more."

Aiden considers this. "Really…" And he undoes the chinstrap, removes the helmet, and tosses a bullseye 20 feet into a nearby trashcan.

"Thanks for the tip!" He starts the big bike and roars off. The two men lock eyes, then frantically scramble to the trashcan to retrieve the castoff, arguing comically for possession.

Aiden has always hated helmets.

The wind blowing through his long brown locks, Aiden feels optimistic. It takes him about ten minutes to get to Best Buy. He secures the bike and enters.

It's like Disneyland to the Irishman. Everything in America is so much bigger, louder, brighter. He buys a Dell Latitude 14 Rugged Extreme. Big, armored, heavy. It sets him back more than two grand. He also picks up a small screwdriver set and some extra RAM for the laptop which he will install back at the motel. He secures his new family member in his locking saddlebag and roars off to the other side of town. He looks at his clock. Almost 9 p.m.

If Aidan needs more proof of the city welcoming him to its bosom, his first home drive-by will provide it. Zeeb road runs about four miles west of town. He slows the bike when he nears the address, finally finding the sign bearing the numbers next to a sturdy mailbox and a large sign that reads FOR SALE BY OWNER. There is no house visible through the tall grasses and bushes, just a long driveway.

Aidan snicks off the headlights and quietly motors down the drive about 200 yards, stopping at the edge of a clearing. He shuts the bike down and beholds his dreamhouse. It's a large ranch-style home with a two-car garage attached. He sits and gawks for a good couple of minutes, then decides to stroll about the place. The moment he is free of the seat and standing tall he hears a metallic click and a stern bass voice.

"Don't even move."

Aiden raises his hands in the air and turns to the sound. The man, a big man, is holding a double-barrel side-by-side shotgun, with confidence and elan that Aidan can sense, pointed directly at the chest of Aiden Bell, standing not 10 yards away.

"Saw you in the security camera coming up the drive. What do you want? There's nothing inside. Everything is moved."

"I want to buy your house," Aidan offers innocently.

The man considers this. "I'd rather we discussed this during daylight hours."

"Let's make an exception."

"I'm asking 350." He notes the confused look on the Irishman's face and politely elaborates. "That's 350,000

American dollars," the big man says, thinking that this datum will put a quick end to the discussion.

"All right."

"But it's a seller's market, you know."

"No. I mean… I don't know what a seller's market is."

The fellow chuckles good-naturedly. "It means I'm likely to get more for it. People bidding on it and such. Could take days." He lowers the gun not an inch.

"Show me around," Aidan says. "If I like the place I'll give you four."

"Four? You mean 400,000 dollars?" He laughs. "Can you get the mortgage?"

"I'll pay you cash. Tomorrow."

"Cash… tomorrow?" The man with the gun considers. "Okay… let's look around. But so far I'm not comfortable laying this shotgun aside."

"I'm all right with that," Aidan says. "You'd be a fool to do otherwise."

But by the hour's end he does lay it down, and the two are now sitting on folding chairs in the empty dining room with a glass of whisky each.

The inside of the house is even more compelling to Aidan than the outside. Modern, clean, perfectly and proudly maintained, and the fellow (whose name is Chester, Chet to his friends) has taste enough so that there need be no emergency repainting or any of that sort of annoying nonsense.

They talk about their lives and enjoy most of the bottle that Chet has opened. Aidan tries to be honest, tells of his childhood and upbringing, his schooling, his music studies at Trinity College—holding back only the details of the last few months and the real reason for his patria-tion to the USA. By midnight it is all a done deal. They will conclude their business on the morrow.

What a glorious night.

2

Aidan has a brother, also his best friend, Liam by name, but at the moment he is an ocean away in a Dublin pub, *The Vessel*, well past closing time. In fact, the sun will soon rise on them there. Liam sits with Wee Dillon, the owner of the pub, both still drunk but having switched to black coffee. Liam rises from his chair and stretches.

"Rrrrrraaaauuuughhhh!" he roars. "Jesus, I'm stiff!"

"And not in the good way," Dillon offers.

"Alas not," Liam confirms. "Time for me to-" and they hear the front door handle being jostled hard from the outside.

Dillion calls out, "It's locked! We're closed! Obviously!"

But the front door gives way from a mighty kick that can only have come from a giant or a battering ram. Wood splinters, and metal shards from the lock and handle spray into the room, and in walks a woman of average size.

Both men are now on their feet, backing toward the wall as she approaches them. Now the two men are backed up to the wall, terrified at the familiar sight of this incredible beauty, red hair and palest skin, jeans and a t-shirt, now standing in front of the two men, each at her arm's length.

"Fiona…" Liam mutters, "what-"

"Where is he?" A voice more like singing than speaking. Heavenly sounds from a fallen angel.

"I don't know! I've told you before, I-"

"I *know* that you know. He's your brother! He's your best friend. And you'll not lie to me any longer Liam Bell."

Liam gets real calm and says, "I can't tell you what I don't know."

Fiona steps closer. She knows he's lying but Liam's loyalty to his brother is legendary. She considers this.

"And you might never tell me no matter how I hurt you, I suppose."

"I suppose that's right," he whispers. "But I'd rather we didn't go that route."

She grins. "But you *will* tell me. You'll tell me or Dillon will die. And it will be your stubbornness that kills him."

Dillon stiffens and stutters. "Me?... Why?... what did I-"

And Fiona shoots out with her left hand and seizes Little Dillon by the throat. And lifts, with her single arm, till Dillon's feet no longer touch the floor, held aloft by a literal death-grip about his throat. He turns red and thrashes in her grip, but she isn't even looking at him. She's looking at Liam, and she's smiling. All this is effortless to her. Dillon is choking, pulling at her hand, punching wildly at her arm, but to no effect. He is turning purple and making animal noises of agony.

"In the next few seconds one of two things will happen, Liam. You will tell me where Aidan is, or poor Dillon will die from your stubbornness."

Dillon has lost consciousness in her grip, and this breaks Liam.

"All right stop! I'll tell!"

She loosens her grip and Dillon falls in a heap. (The nickname 'Little' is pure irony; he's six-foot and easily 300 pounds.) He is alive, but it was a close one.

"Start talking or I finish the job."

"He's in the States."

Fiona is crestfallen. She closes her eyes, hangs her head and is silent for a space. "The bastard… ungrateful bastard."

Dillon comes to and pulls himself up, sitting with his back against the wall, staring at Fiona with a look of frightened wonder.

"Where in the States did he go?"

"I don't know."

Fiona takes an angry step toward Liam, who puts both hands in front of him to ward her off. "I'll tell you what I know. Stay back!"

"Where is he?"

"He said he was going to New York. He wanted to buy a new motorcycle and take it west. That's all he said. Take it west. I swear to Christ that's all he told me. He wants to see America or some shite."

"What's his phone number?"

Liam was told she would ask, that it would be okay to tell her, and he does.

Fiona senses the truth there, turns on her heel and starts toward the door.

"Fiona!" Liam calls. She stops and turns. "Please. Please don't ever come back here. I…" he considers and comes right out with it. "I hate you."

This hurts her. Just a flash as childhood memories are recalled. Liam could tell. She recovers quickly, looks at Liam and spits on the floor in disgust.

"Go to hell," she seethes and turns, walking toward the broken door.

With a bravery mustered from a look at his ravaged friend on the floor beside him, he shouts back, *"I think you beat us there, lass!"*

She never even turns around.

She's famished. And furious.

It's almost dawn and she's feeling uncomfortable at the encroaching twilight, so she needs to act quickly.

People are beginning to avoid her in Dublin. There are rumors.

She used to be such a nice girl. She was considering the convent before it happened. Such a nice family, mostly. A little on the hyper-religious side, and daddy was strict. All the boys loved her, but from a distance, and no one ever bragged about getting near her, you know, in *that* way. But daddy is gone now. Fiona reasons—*he had it coming.* After he 'died,' Fiona vanished and moved to Dublin, to a small home in a cul-de-sac in a rundown part of town. Her mother and brothers, now a hundred miles away, still pine for her and wonder after her.

Tonight she's looking for someone fat and happy, but as daylight threatens she cannot be so choosy. She nears her neighborhood and takes the alley. A few of the pubs along the way are 'lock-ins'—where the drinks flow all the night long for select patrons. Out back in the alleyway is often fertile ground this time of night and so it shall be tonight, or so Fiona intuits.

She spies a young man having a marijuana cigarette with a couple of friends. Fiona slips into the shadows beside a dumpster and waits. Her hunger burns bright tonight, and she mustn't do anything rash or stupid. She mustn't! At last Fiona sees two of his guests re-enter the pub while the young man nurses the stub of the reefer. She makes her move.

The lad spots her and thinks that this is surely the best pot he's ever smoked! He almost gasps at her beauty as she approaches. (She was always a pretty girl, but now she is perfect.) He decides to tell her this. What can he lose? She stops in front of him and smiles adorably.

"Jaysus!" he says. "The closer you get the better you look!"

"Oh go on!" she laughs. "Sure you're just sayin' that."

He gulps. Still not able to assimilate. "No. I mean… really."

"My, *you* are a handsome *man.*" She strokes his cheek. "Do you believe in love at first sight?" she asks coyly.

"Well… I'm not, umm-"

"Well I never did until tonight," she whispers, up close. "Come with me. I live nearby. I don't want your money. I just want you. Tonight."

"You *do?*" He's a good looking lad but clearly not used to this sort of treatment. And he's *really* stoned. Enough, evidently, to believe anything.

"Please," she begs with a whisper, "don't send me away."

"Well…"

"Please," she repeats, feigning anguish. "I couldn't bear it."

And with that she puts her arms around his neck and clasps him to her body. He puts his arms about her, and they join in an intimate embrace. She presses her hips against him. After a moment, the lad pulls his head back and gazes into those big blue eyes.

They kiss. A taste, a promise of what's to come.

"Lead the way," he whispers. She smiles and they stroll the alleyway, hand in hand.

She unlocks her door and they enter her parlor. This is her 'normal room.' It's a prop, like a movie set. It's designed for overstuffed comfort in all the traditional ways and it's easy for visitors to relax in. The only odd feature is the many layers of plastic tarp that cover the middle of the floor. The other three rooms are empty except for her bedroom, which has a single twin-size bed, a side table, and room-darkening shades. The kitchen seems pretty standard, outfitted with a dining table and chairs, and modern, never-used appliances. It's taken a few weeks, but she's got it down!

Fiona locks the door behind her new suitor, takes off her shoes (he does the same) and she pads out to the middle of the room. He follows. She puts her arms around him, and they embrace. He's locked in.

"So!" the lad says. "My name is Sean."

"That's okay," Fiona says. "I don't really care to know that."

Sean is silent for a moment and says, "Well, that's a wee bit odd."

"I suppose," she sighs.

"So then. What do we do now?" he asks, then mumbles, "what's with the plastic on the floor?"

She ignores him, holding him tightly. "Sometimes I like to have sex first. I love sex, you see. But, well, I was in a big rush tonight and you're not really… you're not my type."

"What?" He tries to pull away, but she holds him fast. "What do you mean 'sex first'?"

"Oh, don't get me wrong, John… or… Shannon?"

"Sean!"

"Right. Sorry. Sean," she corrects. "I mean, I'm looking forward to draining you, but not through your willy, if you get me." She chuckles.

He pulls violently away but to no effect whatever. Fiona grabs his hair, tips his head forward and sinks her canines home. He jerks about uselessly, never threatening Fiona's grip on him. She guides him gently to the floor, never breaking the critical contact. He hardly makes a sound through the entire ordeal, which lasts a good three minutes. At last she pulls her head up and takes a deep breath, refreshed and sated.

She enjoys the afterglow, always relaxing, which is enhanced by all the marijuana in her latest meal. She sits with her back to the big sofa for the better part of an hour and finally observes the dawn sunlight flickering in through a small gap in the shades. She rises with grace and stretches her perfect body.

Poor Sean is already positioned perfectly on the tarp. All she has to do is gather up a layer of plastic and roll him up tight. With that she goes to the kitchen to get the ties and secures her bundle. After a long, well-earned sleep, Fiona will toss the corpse into the trunk of her Volvo and take a pleasant drive out to her disposal site— which is starting to fill up. She needs to think about that.

Fiona believes she knows why Aidan left her, and why he left Ireland. The country is too small, even a city like Dublin, to let pass unnoticed so many missing people, so many found corpses so oddly mutilated: drained of blood with holes in their throats.

He must have felt the heat, she thinks, *as I'm starting to sense it myself. I must be suspected. They must have some idea by now. Do the guards think it's a complicated prank by a serial killer and they're somehow managing to keep it all under wraps? Or do some suspect the truth? That we are not just a legend. I know why Aidan left these shores. In the States the pickings are easy! So many people. So many cities dense with prey. So many places to hide away.* She chuckles, and then turns sad. *And, of course, he left because he hates and fears me. But I know he'll love me again. When he finally accepts what he has become, he will love me again!*

She knows she must follow. Not just to escape these shores, but to find Aidan, to recover the only thing she has ever loved—a man who can still her storms with a touch; in whom she finds her only solace; the antidote to hate and rage; the sole link to her girlish innocence and the only gentle thing.

The bastard. The ungrateful bastard.

Liam never went home. He and Wee Dillon are sipping fresh hot coffee at a table in the pub. While Dillon recovered from his strangulation ordeal, Liam heaved the heavy front door back near its original position and taped a sign on the busted door to the effect that the pub is closed.

"I'll call Flynn in a couple hours," Dillon says, his voice weak and raspy.

"What? Flynn... Mike Flynn? Oh, about the door. Good idea," Liam says. "Hope he can get to it today."

"Well, he'd better or I'm fucked."

They sit in glum silence for a minute.

Dillon whispers. "What a crazy bitch..."

Liam meets Wee Dillon's eyes and Dillon bursts into tears. It's been a terrible day and it isn't even nine in the morning.

"Jesus, Dillon..." Liam says. "I'm sorry all this happened to you."

Dillon recovers quickly, wipes tears from his face and looks embarrassed. "Ah... fuck all."

They sip their java.

"Can you call Aidan?" Dillon asks Liam. "You know she'll come for him."

"I'll warn him. Maybe she won't find him."

"Ahh… but you know she'll try." They consider this. "She'll kill him!"

"I said I'll call him. And I dunno if she'll kill him or not. Aidan's smart." Liam waves a slow hand about the pub. "It's not like we don't have our own worries." (Liam is the cook at *The Vessel,* and shares in the profits and losses.)

"Well… one thing for certain," Dillon says. "She needs to go. There'll be lots fewer unexplained deaths and missing persons in Ireland. It's getting ridiculous!"

3

There is nothing, absolutely nothing, that Aidan doesn't love about his new home. It's been but a week, but everything is in place.

Aidan's home in Ann Arbor

His big bike is paired with a new Subaru Outback in the garage, ready for the fabled Michigan winter. The cavernous living room has a new seven-foot Steinway B in the center, flanked by two giant Magnaplanar loud-speakers for the new stereo, with comfort provided by two big sofas and two La-Z-Boys, a couple of long coffee tables in front of the sofas, and a side table each for the recliners.

There's a TV room, with a 70-inch screen and a view-ing couch for three. His master bedroom has a king-sized bed, desk and chair, and the other two bedrooms are empty.

The kitchen has the appliances that came with the house, but only the refrigerator will see any use—he'll stow beer for the odd guest, maybe some wine, and vodka for himself in the freezer.

The sustenance problem has been the only real difficulty. He's eaten only half of what he is accustomed to. He's pale and low in energy. He has only fed twice in the past week and both meals were hard to come by. Aiden searched for the high-crime areas and found slim pickings in Ann Arbor or westward. He has decided to visit the adjacent city to the east of Ann Arbor, Ypsilanti, to try his luck tonight.

The bars (are supposed to) close at 2:30 a.m. in Michigan. Aidan will discover that 2:30 to 3:30 will be the 'golden hour' for a quick meal in the wrong part of town, and this will come in handy often. He waits impatiently now, looks at his watch, sees 12:46 a.m., and tries not to think about how famished he feels. He decides to head out.

Easy meals are a mixed blessing, Aidan has long known. It's easy to lure someone to attack him in a bad neighborhood at 3 a.m., and it's filling and sustaining, but this sort of blood is always tainted with who-knows-what. Alcohol, marijuana, cocaine, heroin, meth—a long list of probabilities. He is incalculably stronger in constitution than even his most toxic of victims, and his metabolism is rarely insulted to the point of true unease, but these cheapest of thrills exact a price that he's sick of paying.

It hurts him to remember the sweet blood of sweet people, back when he was new, when he had none of the moral constraint that he has now. Like cold, fresh water from a crystal brook that slaked the thirst so completely, all so voluptuous and gratifying. The children were the finest of all, but there is no thought, no memory he can conjure that sickens him as much as this, to relive those moments, the stuff of his nightmares and the source of his self-loathing. (They're so small—sometimes he would need two.) He tells himself that he had no choice, the insanity of the newborn rages so completely that the concept of self-control is simply an impossibility. But was this really true? Or was the pleasure so deep and all-consuming that he simply forgot all else?

He pointed the big Beemer to a neighborhood north of Ypsi that, according to his reference, offered good hunting. (He would only *seem* to be the prey.) Tonight, the bait is his bike.

He dismounts in front of an abandoned storefront and begins a little stroll, the unattended bike never out of sight. It doesn't take long for a carload of young men to tool by, slowing down as they spy the bike. Loud hip-hop blares distorted noises from the car stereo. The car continues another 100 yards or so, then turns around. Someone shuts the music off. They slow down as they approach the big bike and pull in a few yards from it. This is Aidan's cue to walk back and join the scene.

Three men, in their 20s it seems to Aidan, hop out of the old Buick, and stand next to the bike. One of the men spies Aidan crossing the street, walking toward them. They face him as a wall. The one in the middle, the big one, speaks.

"This here motorcycle belong to you?"

Aidan stops a few feet from the men, just out of reach. "Yep."

The one on the right turns his head and spits to the ground. He turns back to Aidan. "What are you doin' here, man?"

Aidan smiles. "Just going for a wee stroll. Nice night."

"And I suppose you gonna hop your horse and go for a drive now? Dat right?" From the man in the middle.

"You too far from home, bitch," says the man who spit.

The silent man reaches to the small of his back and pulls a shiny, long knife, and grins at Aidan with a half-toothless smile, waving the big blade back and forth. A car drives by, a driver and passenger. They look, they don't even slow down. They know the neighborhood.

Aidan flashes out with his left hand and snatches the knife out of the grinning fool's hand. Aidan stands now, smiling at the three men, who look at one another in amazement. Aidan throws the knife behind him, well out of the way.

The three rush upon Aidan as one.

Now, Aidan is not so much interested in 'winning the fight' as he is to choose wisely among the three. The grinning fool is very intoxicated, slow and clumsy; the big man in the middle fights with a sort of rage that Aidan has recognized in meth-heads, it's unnatural, he can smell it; the spitter fights with style and grace, and Aidan cannot detect so much as a trace of alcohol in his aura.

Decision made, Aidan dispatches the other two with punches in the head that KO'd the pair instantly. Now it's just Aidan and Spitter, who is not just a graceful opponent, but smart enough to know that he hasn't a chance.

"Okay... okay... you win, man," he says, backing away from Aidan and desperately winded. Aidan relaxes, disappointed and determined to show mercy to the supplicant, but Spitter flashes out with a sneaky right jab at Aidan's head, not understanding that Aidan sees this as we might see a boxing scene in slow motion. Aidan is on him in a flash. He places his left arm around Spitter and grabs his hair with his right hand, tilting aside his head.

"You fought well," Aidan says, and these are the last words that Spitter hears.

In his afterglow, Aidan is sitting on the ground, leaning against his bike. He had dragged the three bodies out of sight of the road so he could bask without worry in his post-feeding bliss. There was no booze and no drugs that Aidan could sense in that splendid meal. He had chosen well; his most satisfying repast since he arrived on these shores. Cars drove by, expressing no interest. It was almost 3:30 a.m. Time for a nice drive home, where he could enjoy some reading until sunrise, then sleep.

4

Fiona decides to take a cruise ship to New York because she always wanted to be on a boat, and because all her victims can be thrown unobserved into the sea.

Aidan's brother, Liam, wants to be with his brother. He will fly in an airplane, like a normal human. Wee Dillon wants to come with, but he's trying to run a pub. His livelihood and his community depend upon it. Liam won't hear of it. Dillon will have to find another cook.

5

Aidan remains unsettled in two very urgent ways: First, he needs to find a reliable source of relatively wholesome human blood. He understands that the ecstasy of feeding on innocents is disallowed him forever, and he's okay with that, but the tainted blood of drug addicts and boozers is finally starting to really impact his quality of life.

Secondly, but almost as urgent, is that Aiden needs to work. He gets bored easily. He wants to try teaching, maybe even performing. Why not? His papers from Trinity College are in order. He has many private recordings and good references. He decides that, starting tomorrow, he will start to call and assess the needs of the local universities.

But the food issue needs attention, and quickly. After spending all night analyzing the problem he almost gave up, resigning himself to his current unsavory regimen. But just at the point of surrender, it happens, as it so often does, that Aidan has an inspiring idea. He opens his laptop and starts to research.

Aidan knows that in Ireland there is a register of sex offenders, but the public is disallowed from viewing it. (He first had this idea back in Dublin but saw that was untenable.) But here in the USA, here in Michigan, that list is *public*. Aidan conceives of a grand plan that will not only feed him for months to come, but he will be doing a public service for the good citizens of Michigan. The recidivism rate of sex offenders is appalling, and Aidan is in a position to do what the law cannot: remove these people from all future temptations and ensure the safety of the innocents in his community. *Aidan Bell, public servant.* He laughs.

He bookmarks the relevant websites, closes his laptop, and looks at the clock. Sunrise soon. It has been a most fruitful night, but now he must consider strategy and tactics, something he has always enjoyed.

6

You can take the girl out of the trailer park, but
you can't take the trailer park out of the girl.
— an American axiom

It will take seven days for the good ship *Cunard Queen Mary 2* to take Fiona to New York City. She is excited. She has left Ireland only once and that just recently and has never even seen much of her homeland.

Cunard Queen Mary 2

She had to shop for the trip! She enjoyed that considerably. Growing up in near-poverty in the Irish outback instilled little fashion sense into the girl. Clothing that approximately fit without too much wear and tear was the best she could hope for. Now, Fiona shall be the most beautiful woman on board the *Queen Mary*, even without the garish and audacious clothes she's picked out. Someone needs to dress this girl because she has money now but very little in the way of sophistication.

7

Fiona was one of three children in her shanty-Irish family and attended Catholic school, staying close to the Church, and serving as housekeeper in the priest's rectory until the change came upon her at age 19.

She had a classmate, Aidan Bell, from a lace-curtain Irish family who lived over the hill. The Bells were the only wealthy family in that part of the county. They lived well but very modestly, sending their children to the local Catholic school.

Fiona and Aidan had known one another since the third class when they were both ten years-old. Fiona was a girly-girl and a bit of an air-head (though these two features need not occur together), and Aidan felt protective toward her. He was a gallant lad, always respectful and keen on his studies, unlike his year-younger brother Liam, who was a scamp and a scoundrel from toddlerhood.

As the years passed the pair grew close. Aidan knew there were many tensions in Fiona's family. Dad was strict, a bully and a drunkard. Mom was submissive and though she tried to protect Fiona from her father's brutish ways, the frequent cuts and bruises gave the lie to mom's efforts. The abuse was as hard on Aidan as it was on Fiona, perhaps worse. She would unburden herself to him, but it would be gentle Aidan who would collapse in empathic tears, not Fiona. To her, this was simply how life was.

Aidan felt helpless. Fiona's father was large and pugnacious, a frequent brawler at local pubs with a hair-trigger temper when he was in his cups. Aidan was a skinny kid, and Fiona's father could break him in half with little effort. Fiona had fallen in love with Aidan long before puberty, and when she had murdered her father at age 20 she did it more to avenge Aidan's agonies than her own.

Aidan's love was as a brother who loved a little sister he never had; Fiona's love was romantic and would become a passionate devotion. And there was the rub that would spark the climax of their existence.

The skinny boy that was Aidan grew to become a sturdy, lean young man. He and Fiona saw one another frequently throughout their school years, and life became better for Fiona at home because her father had suffered a stroke that debilitated him, not completely, but enough so that he was no longer a physical threat to Fiona or her mother.

Fiona had a pious streak. Her Catholic education had always kept her unquestioningly in line. She was devout, praying the Rosary and attending daily Mass—habits she had kept all through school and then, in her 19th year, she was offered the housekeeping position at the parish rectory. This brought needed income to her family and kept her busy six days a week.

The parish priest was a kindly man, a Father FitzGerald. A month after he had engaged Fiona in her housekeeping job, Father Fitz (as he was known) passed from a heart attack in his sleep. The parish would not have a new pastor assigned for a month, so a temporary priest was brought in to fill the gap, a Father Kevin O'Doul.

Father Kevin was a monster in disguise (such a perfect disguise), and he became spellbound by the sweet and guileless Fiona. She would complain about him to Aidan. They sat outside on the porch of Aiden's house, watching the sunset.

"I know I only have to stick it out for another week, but Father Kevin is kind of a letch, I think," she told him.

"Why? What does he do?"

"Well…" this was hard for her. "He paws me. It's all so fatherly and affectionate and then it's all squeezy and rubby. And the way he looks at me… it's…"

"Maybe I should have a word with him. Or you should tell your brothers."

She jumped at this. "No, my God, no," she gasped. "I don't want to make a big thing of this! I need my job! It's only another week."

Aiden agreed to stay out of it, but he decided to try to keep tabs on her. Somehow.

The night before Father Kevin was to finally leave the parish, passing the baton to another priest who would be permanently assigned, Fiona was in the kitchen washing her dinner dishes. (Father Kevin never ate at the rectory. This lightened her workload considerably and she enjoyed the break.) Father Kevin entered and greeted her.

"Fiona, dear," he began. "I have a small present for you, to give to you before I leave. I'll be gone tomorrow morning before the sun is up."

Fiona was uncomfortable. She has no idea what she should do. She simply stares back at Father Kevin with a small smile.

"Come walk with me, out in the yard. That will be a fitting place to give you your gift. You've taken good care of me in my stay, and I will show you my appreciation." It wasn't a request. It was an order. Fiona always felt almost mesmerized in the power of his presence but had the wit to have a care.

"Well… of course, Father Kevin," she said. "But I have to visit the bathroom."

"I'll meet you on the back porch," he said, and was off.

Fiona ran to the bathroom, closed the door, and rang Aidan on her cellphone. He picked up.

"Aidan!"

"Fiona. Something wrong?"

"I dunno. Father Kevin wants me to walk with him in the yard. He says he has a present for me."

"On my way," Aidan said.

"Aidan?... Aidan?" he had hung up. Fiona sighed, washed her face, and went out to face the music.

She met the priest out back, and he gallantly offered her his arm, which she took graciously but he could sense her reluctance. They began to stroll in silence in the yard—a great plot of well-tended grass, with many, many gravestones and simple markers. They stopped about 50 yards from the rectory.

Fiona's fateful churchyard

"Ah," he said. "This will do nicely."

Fiona was terrified. *Nicely for what?*

"Let's sit on the grass," he said and did, and she followed. The evening was very warm and breezy. "I want you to know a little about me before I give you your gift."

"Oh… okay then," she squeaked.

"You will not believe what I am going to tell you. At least not at first, but when we leave here it will become clear. Understand?"

"No. I mean… as much as I can, I suppose."

"I am 351 years-old." He waited for her reaction. Nothing. She sat with downcast eyes.

"There are no others like me in Ireland, and there have been none for two centuries. When I met you, I recognized you."

"As what?" she blurted.

"As one who shall become as me."

Fiona tried to stand, to flee, but he caught her ankle and held it fast. She struggled until she knew the futility of it and then settled down. Then she began to cry. He released her foot and sat himself closer to her. He touched her shoulder and she startled.

"Come, come," he said in a consoling voice. "There's no need for tears. I promise you. I promise you shall see." She calmed a bit. "May I continue?" he asked. Fiona nodded. "You shall be one of the immortals."

"What does that mean?" she whispered.

"Well," he laughed, "that's what we call ourselves"

"Please… please don't hurt me," she pleaded pathetically.

"I'm here to give you life eternal, not to hurt you."

"But Jesus gives us life eternal already." She starts to weep again, softly.

"This is different," he said. "For after tonight you will not age. You will be even more perfectly lovely than you are now and never suffer sickness or decay. Boundless strength and energy will be yours, reflexes to shame a jungle cat, eyesight to shame an eagle, lightning speed, godlike endurance. Is that not exciting?"

"I don't know… I'm so confused." Her weeping had stopped. She just sat, inert, knowing she was completely in his power and waiting.

"Before the transition, I will take your virginity. It is irresistible. It cries out to me."

At this Fiona screamed and tried to thrash away in escape.

"*Stop!*" he demanded. And she did. She sat still and ramrod straight.

He gathered her dress at the bottom and pulled it up to the top of her thighs.

"Lift your bottom," he instructed, and she complied. He lifted the dress free, then worked it up, and as she raised her arms he lifted the dress over her head and cast it aside. Her face showed no emotion. He leaned over so that he could manipulate her bra from behind and un-hooked it. He sat up, grabbed the bra in front and waited a moment as she straightened her arms so he could pull it free. He tossed this aside.

"Lift your bottom," he repeated, and he slipped her knickers down her thighs, over her knees, down her calves and off. He tossed these on the pile. She was now naked in the light of a half-moon, which was much brighter to Father Kevin than to a mere mortal. More than bright enough. He beheld her.

"How unimaginably lovely you are," he said.

She looked at him and blinked, as if she were begin-ning to comprehend something impossibly deep.

"I am?"

"You are. Lie down."

He explored every inch of her, front and back, with kisses and caresses. He finally ordered her to get on hands and knees and he entered her from behind. She was passive and made barely a sound throughout the entire ordeal, as if spellbound. In a short time he climaxed, slumped over her, and kissed her back.

When at last he withdrew she gasped at the gesture. The scent hit him first, like a velvet hammer. He steadied Fiona in her place and noticed that there was a bit of blood on both their genitals. She was a virgin, indeed.

The priest dabbed gently at her most private areas and slowly brought a smear of her blood to his tongue. Eyes closed, he savored her essence. He gazed up at the dazzling white moon, shuddered, and moaned aloud, stirred to his very core.

When at last he recovered, he instructed Fiona to lie down on her back and she complied. He scrutinized her face. She looked like a child. There was only a blank calm, no anger, no upset. Finally, she spoke in a flat voice.

"Was that my gift?"

He laughed. "No, dearest. That was a gift from myself to myself. Your gift is here," And as he leaned his head into her neck the heavy iron spade of a shovel bashed into the back of his head. In a flash he was on his feet, staring into the enraged face of Aidan Bell.

"That *hurt!*" the priest growled.

Aidan is aghast. "How can you… how can you even stand up?"

The mad priest stepped toward Aidan who cocked his arm for another shovel-blow, but Fiona, naked as a nymph, was on her feet and cried out.

"Father Kevin, stop!"

He stopped his advance and turned to her.

"I don't care what you do to me, but please, I beg you, I *beg* you, don't harm Aidan. He's just looking out for me."

The priest laughed. In a flash he was next to Aidan and *he had the shovel in his hand*. He tapped Aidan on the side of the head with it and the lad went down for the count.

Fiona screamed. The priest was at her in an instant with his hand covering her mouth. She calmed in seconds and he released her.

"He'll be all right," he said. "In a few hours."

"Thank you," she said, flooded with relief. The priest embraced her, and she did not resist.

He unclasped her and said, "Let us continue."

Fiona walked slowly back to her former spot and lay down. Father Kevin sat beside her, gazed lovingly into her eyes for almost a minute, then bent to kiss her breasts and fondle the sweet flesh, impressing this innocent mortal beauty, this unimaginable loveliness into his mind, never to be forgotten and often recalled through the centuries to come. She lay there, impassive. As he leaned into her neck his canine teeth became elongated and razor sharp.

He was not feeding here, not merely, though the savor was exquisite. He imbibed an elixir of such purity and angelic perfection he had never before known. He was on a delicate mission. He had taken half his usual quota of blood and withdrew. He studied her. She looked delirious.

He reached into his pants pocket and withdrew his penknife, opened it, and with it he carefully nicked at the artery in his wrist. As it spouted blood he held his wrist to Fiona's mouth, and she sucked at it. At first very tentatively, then all of a sudden her eyes widened, and the girl grabbed at his hand, sitting up and repositioning the spouting wound that she might suck harder and faster, all the while bucking and twisting. He cried out. This was agonizing for him. At last he knew he must stop her, but she would not be turned. It took tremendous force to break this connection.

He held a handkerchief to his now gushing wrist. It would bleed for most of the night. He would have to feed tomorrow.

So would Fiona.

8

Liam beat Fiona to New York by a month, flights from Dublin vastly outnumbering the departures of luxury cruise liners. Aidan asked him if he needed money. Of *course* Liam needed money. Liam *always* needs money, but he has never taken a cent from Aidan and won't now. Liam has agreed to stay (at least until the inevitable confrontation with Fiona) at Aidan's Ann Arbor home during his visitation. Both brothers are pleased with this plan.

Liam took a bus from New York City to Ann Arbor. It cost less than $70 and took about 20 grueling hours, screaming babies included free-of-charge. Aidan met him at the old bus terminal in the heat of the mid-afternoon. He picked Liam up on his new bike, dressed in leather from neck to toe, and crowned with Aidan's day-helmet. This was a full-coverage affair with a face-shield so dark it appeared black. Sunlight could not invade this costume.

They had a little lunch, Aidan's treat. Liam had a corned beef sandwich and a Guinness.

"Why does this taste not like Guinness?" Liam asked his brother.

"Welcome to America," Aidan answered. He had a vodka martini. Then it was to the party store and back to the house. They both needed a nap.

"The jet-lag is bustin' me balls," Liam says over a frosty glass of Harp, sitting in one of the recliners in the living room.

Aiden laughs. He misses his brother's humor.

It is almost 10 p.m. This is when Aiden usually wakes, but he realizes things are going to have to change. Concordia College needed a professor of piano and Aidan pretty much walked right into it. His interview, credentials, references, recordings, and a brief impromptu recital easily carrying the day. Further proof of how welcoming Ann Arbor is to the Irish newcomer. But it will play havoc with his sleeping schedule.

"When do you start?" Liam asks.

"Three days. Monday," he says.

"Did they advertise for a vampire, or just a piano teacher?" smartassed Liam asks.

"You think I should tell them?" And they both laugh. Liam takes another hit of his beer and looks serious now.

"How do you feed here? Must be easier than Dublin. I think you got out just in time."

Liam nods. "I think I did, too. I was feeding on the usual lowlife, mainly in the city next door, but... too many drug addicts. Too many drunks with God knows what else mixed in. It gets debilitating. I have a new plan."

"Which is?"

"I start tomorrow night, actually." He pauses. It's a strange thing to talk about, even to Liam. "I'm going to eat child molesters," he says proudly.

Liam perks up. "Like a public service?"

"Aye!" Aidan shouts. "Just what I thought!" And they laugh long and hard.

"How do you find them?" Liam asks.

"Get this: In America, they not only publish a list on the internet, *they have pictures and addresses!"*

Liam is skeptical. "Ah, go on... pull the other one."

"No, I'm not joking. I'll show you."

"So you picked a guy out? I mean, they're blokes, right?"

"Almost all. It would be too depressing to do a woman like that."

"I suppose... but you have someone in mind for tomorrow?"

"I do indeed."

Liam has always found it uncomfortable to dig too deeply into the nitty-gritty of his brother's life and habits, especially dietary, so he leaves off.

"Well, let me know how it goes."

"Will do. Another beer? I'm going to make a nice drink for myself."

"Aye. Thank you. Many more beers. And bring the crisps!"

"Chips. Chips they call 'em here. And they call chips French Fries. Can you believe that?"

"What in fuck do the French have to do with a fried stick of potato? Silly yanks..."

"I know. Lots of strange stuff here."

"And bring those American pretzels, too!"

9

She knows *just* what to wear. She is *so* excited.

It's red, and very short, and strapless, and backless. And it has all these frills, and this bow! It's gorgeous! Like nothing she's ever had in her entire life.

She's so flawless, she could wear an old shower curtain and it wouldn't take away from her essential perfection, but the QM2 crowd is not a gaggle of back country Irish yokels. She'll discover this tonight at the ball, though the painful lesson will have a silver lining.

As she enters the ballroom, all eyes are on her. But she notices that although the men seem enchanted, most of the women are sniggering, pointing, or even outright laughing. This embarrasses Fiona. She blushes as she sits alone at her table along the wall of the ballroom. She orders gin on the rocks. The band, a dozen or so players, are warming up and conversing.

She needs to feed tonight, having only fed once so far on the ship, an action which has caused much commotion and anxiety among the passengers. Her victim, a wolfish young man who was not as good a lover as he promised he'd be, had simply vanished from the boat!

After their liaison had concluded, which Fiona perceived as too short and too selfish on his part, she wanted to stroll the lonely 4 a.m. decks of the ship. Loverboy reluctantly agreed. When they came to the spot Fiona had scouted out she began to tell him off in vivid terms, almost reducing him to a jelly of tears after berating his skills and his manhood in general. Her tirade concluded, she knocked him down and fed vengefully upon him. When she was finished, she stood, grabbed him by the ankle and spun him about like a helicopter blade, finally releasing him in a high slow trajectory into the sea.

But Fiona was not careful, as she so often is not. Instead of simply tossing him overboard, she flung him in her rage high and long, *and there were witnesses.* A few. They all told the same story of the missing man flying through the air into the ocean. This has launched an investigation, but saucy Fiona is unconcerned. How could they even guess?

That was three nights ago. She hopes for a more fulfilling liaison this evening though she spies so far no unattached males among the attendees. Two tables down she sees a handsome young man sitting with two women, one enjoying her drink and the other whispering to the young man while staring at Fiona. Fiona is uncomfortable. And angry. Why is she being singled out this way?

The young man pushes up from his chair and walks over to Fiona. She looks up as if bothered a bit by his presumption.

"Won't you join us?" He says. "I mean… unless you're waiting for someone. It's not right to sit alone at the ball."

Fiona is disarmed. The young man is sincere.

He extends his hand. "My name is Oliver. Yours?"

"Umm… Fiona."

"Come join us, Fiona."

She does. He escorts her to the table and pulls a chair out for her. She sits, enjoying the courtesy.

"Let me introduce Caroline and Dinah. This is Fiona."

"A pleasure to meet you both," Fiona says. Caroline smiles; Dinah grins.

"Oh, you're Irish," Caroline says. "You have a lovely voice."

"Thank you."

Dinah can't hold back. "Tell me, where did you get your dress?"

Fiona looks down, as if seeing it for the first time. "Oh! I picked it up in Dublin before I sailed."

"I think it's charming," Oliver says.

"I'm sure you do," Dinah drones.

Fiona is a bit ruffled. "Dinah? Dinah is it?"

Dinah nods.

"Is there something wrong with how I look?"

"Oh no! No." she can barely stifle a laugh. "Not at 'tall," she says, in a parody of Fiona's brogue.

"Cool it," Caroline whispers to Dinah. "Have another drink."

"Yes," Oliver says. "More drinks!" He snaps a finger at a waiter. "What will you have, Fiona?"

"A gin on ice, please."

Oliver instructs the server, who gives a little bow and scurries away.

"So," Oliver says, "what do you do in Ireland, Fiona?"

"Whatever I wish," she says, smiling.

"Professionally?"

"Nothing," she says, without a hint of insecurity.

Oliver points to the ladies. "Like these two," he laughs. "Unless you count spending their way through fortunes a profession."

Caroline laughs. *She has a good nature*, Fiona observes. *Dinah doesn't.*

"Oh fuck you, Olly," Dinah says. "Just because you work for a living."

Oliver brushes it aside. "I love my work. And you're one of the beneficiaries, so be nice."

"What is it you do?" Fiona asks.

"Television wardrobe," he replies. Fiona looks confused. "I dress actors on television shows."

"He's the best!" Caroline pips.

Fiona wonders. She points at one, then the other. "Are you two…"

"What!" Caroline laughs. "O god no. Not for years."

"We had a torrid romance, what 10, 12 years ago?"

"12," Caroline confirms.

"We're old friends now," he says.

Fiona looks at Dinah, hoping there is no connection there.

"Don't look at *me,*" she says. "He's not my type."

"Good," Fiona says, losing patience with this woman. "I can't imagine that you're *his* type."

Dinah looks like she's been slapped and gropes for a retort but comes up empty. Fiona laughs. *Bitch.*

Fiona's hunting grounds on the QM2

The band has started playing. It's an introduction to *Stormy Weather.* Oliver asks Fiona to dance. She is thrilled but won't show it. They walk to the dance floor arm in arm.

"No one writes intros to songs anymore," Oliver says. "But they had a purpose back in the day. Back when people danced." They stop and he puts a hand about her waist and lifts her right hand with his left. The classic starting position.

"What's the purpose, then?" Fiona asks.

"It gave people time to recognize the song and to get to the dance floor with their partner by the time the intro concluded."

"Ah," she says. They begin to sway.

Fiona has never slow-danced before. Never once, but you would never know it. Such grace and anticipation of her partner's lead. They fit beautifully. They speak not a word throughout the song, which was played very well. When it ends he releases her and steps back. They smile their enjoyment at one another.

A new song begins. A fast song. Oliver hollers to the bandstand.

"Mitch!"

The music stops.

"Hey Olly," what's up?" the leader, one of three sax players shouts back, sensing impending improprieties.

"Another slow one, eh?"

"O-li-verrrr..." the leader sounds threatening.

"Just this once. C'mon Mitch. I'll owe you."

"You already owe me." And he steps back, giving new instructions to the band.

They strike up Gershwin's *Someone to Watch Over Me.*

"Ah," Oliver takes Fiona once again in his arms and whispers to her. "Good choice, Mitch."

"Do you always order the band around?" Fiona asks.

Oliver laughs. "Very rarely on these cruises I ask Mitch a favor. I'll owe him big for this one. He truly hates when I do that."

"Well then," Fiona whispers, "I better make it worth your while." She tightens her embrace of Oliver, and he responds in kind. Halfway through the song, Olly pulls his head back and looks at Fiona, into her sky blue eyes.

"Let me dress you," he says.

She breaks with him, looks at him, then down at her dress.

"Jaysus, is it that bad?"

"Listen," he says. "You're the most beautiful woman on the boat. At *least* that. But you need… *help* with your wardrobe. I can help. It's what I *do*. I can teach you to dress yourself in a way that will have you thanking me for the rest of your life. You'll be my greatest achievement."

She doesn't know whether to knock him flat on his arse or kiss him.

"Please, Fiona, don't feel insulted. I would never insult you. I think you know that already." She does. "What have you got to lose? Silly bitches like Dinah… listen, there are tons of them out there just like her. Your beauty makes her jealous, but your dress sense gives her a way to drag you down and pull herself up. Don't let that happen. It's not necessary."

The music stops and an obnoxious jazz arrangement of a rock tune commences. Mitch and Oliver lock glances. Mitch sticks out his tongue vulgarly and Olly laughs. The two dancers head to an unoccupied table and sit.

"How would you start with me?" she wonders.

"Well… we could start on board. But *just* for starters. We'll do our best work in New York. The shops here aren't what they used to be, but we can take a look to-morrow morning. What do you say?"

Fiona agrees. She simply must have sex with this lovely man as quickly as possible and is wondering how to avoid any more delay without appearing to be the slut that at heart she knows she is. She laughs at the thought.

"What's so funny?" Oliver asks.

"Do you want to be alone with me?" she asks. "I've danced enough."

He smiles. "Your voice is so beautiful. It sorts so well with the rest of you." And he kisses her.

They adjourn to his stateroom.

They play in bed for hours. *This is more like it,* Fiona thinks. She is so looking forward to a fling in New York with this wonderful guy.

It's 3 a.m. Oliver is fast asleep, but Fiona has been sleeping all day. And she's hungry.

She slips out of bed, tiptoes to the cabin door, and treads three doors down to Dinah's cabin. (Oliver told her where it is.) She knocks on the door and a light switches on. She waits, and the door opens a crack.

"What the fuck? Fiona? What the hell are you doing here? What time-"

And Fiona bursts in. She clamps Dinah by the throat to silence any noises, kicks the door closed and drags the girl back to her bed, laying her flat. Fiona, still holding Dinah by the throat, sits on her thighs.

Fiona punches her face with her free fist. *"You. Fucking. Bitch!"* She wants to continue but it's pointless— the girl is out cold. She bends to her throat and begins to feed. She drains her to the last possible drop.

That was so delicious in so many ways! Rarely has she had such a satisfying meal. She falls to the bed next to her drained prey and savors the moment. Many blissful minutes go by. She almost nods off and catches herself, then has a buzz-killing thought.

The cleanup. Always the goddamn cleanup. What must I do with her now? she wonders. And then comes to a perfect Fiona-style decision: *Bugger them all. Let her lay in her bed. Let's see what they make of it.* And she tiptoes out of Dinah's cabin and resumes unobserved her cuddle next to the wonderful Oliver, who has so much to teach her! They will both be shocked, shocked! by the terrible news of Dinah's murder the next morning.

What kind of world are we living in!

10

"Do you think you can avoid her?" Liam asks. The beer is gone and so are the pretzels and crisps, eh, chips. The lads are drunk and beat and can't last much longer.

"I don't *want* to avoid her," Aidan says.

Liam is incredulous. "Well, what the hell did you come to the States for?"

"To start over," he says. "I'm not the same man. It's all different for me now. And the way I have to live... Ireland is too small."

"But you can still avoid her if you want to."

"It needs to happen, brother," Aidan says. "Besides. She's on her way."

"You don't know that. And she has no idea where you are."

"Liam. Do you still have your old cellphone?"

He's confused. "Aye. Why?"

"Then Fiona knows *exactly* where we are."

"You mean... she can track my phone?"

"She knows your number, and if she doesn't she can coerce it from someone. Tracking a cellphone that you know the number of isn't exactly rocket surgery. I was going to tell you to turn your location services off on your phone, but then I got to thinking. I could probably avoid her. But there's something else working here. I don't want to be looking over my shoulder for the rest of my life—which could be very long! Also... I need the confrontation. I need it settled."

"Still. I should leave then!"

"Liam, the confrontation is *necessary*. Just be careful and don't get in her way. She'll kill you just to spite me.

And if she confronts you somewhere and you get a chance, give me a heads-up."

They head for bed. Sleep will be difficult—they're both drunk, Liam is jetlagged, and Aidan is way off his schedule.

It's now Saturday afternoon and Aidan must get something to eat. He's going forward with his new plan. His first attempt will be local. If it works out, he'll widen his area to include the Detroit suburbs. Lots of opportunities there and he can spread the heat out to avoid Ann Arbor as a focus.

His intended target is 48 year-old man from the south side of town. Warren Radcliff is his name. Aidan waits until sunset and hops in the Subaru. The car blends in. In Ann Arbor every other car is a Subaru. (The others are Priuses and Teslas.) Aidan needs to draw as little attention as possible to himself. He thought about taking the bike, as he is much more nimble on it and trusts his powers of evasion with it when things get hairy. But the notion of blending in won the day.

He spots the house and slows down, lowering the car windows. He stops in front of the target home and senses no activity. Likewise with the two flanking houses. They are, however, pretty close together, so the ruckus must be kept to a minimum. The neighborhood is very quiet. He drives around the block and parks there, gets out and heads to his intended victim's home.

He is dressed in a white shirt, nice pants, and a his only sportscoat. Aidan looks respectable, almost official. He steps up to the porch and knocks.

"William Radcliff?" he calls.

In a few seconds, a small skinny barefoot fellow in bermudas and a wife-beater t-shirt looks through the peep-hole and assesses Aidan. He opens the door.

"Can I help you?"

Aidan enters without an invitation. Radcliff is too stunned to react before Aidan turns to close the door.

His hunger urges him on to dally as little as possible and he seizes the wee man by both his upper arms and holds him fast.

"Who... Whaddaya want?!" Radcliff eyes pop out like a cartoon character and Aidan chuckles.

"You're a fucking child molester and I'm going to kill you, you pervert fuck," Aidan explains.

"Child molester? I ain't no child molester!"

"What?" *Is this always going to happen?* Aidan wonders.

"I know why you think that! 'Cause I'm on that stupid list! Listen: A girl a month from her 16th birthday tells me she's 18 and begs me to let her blow me for $20 so she could buy drugs!" he cries. "And I was stupid enough to fall for it! That's all I did. And you wanna *kill* me over that?"

Aidan considers this new data.

"And you shoulda seen her! No way she looked like a minor! I *regret* it. It was *stupid*. But I don't do that stuff, getting whores and such. Not no more. I paid my dues. Do all my probation and reporting stuff. Please, buddy." And he starts to cry, then blubbers, "Please..."

"Prove it," Aidan says, and releases his arms.

He stops crying and wipes his nose. "Follow me."

They enter his bedroom where he opens a desk drawer, removes a folder and riffles through it to find a single sheet of paper which he hands to Aidan. Aidan reads. Radcliff turns back to the drawer and puts the folder back. He does not close the drawer.

But there it is in black and white and a government seal. Statutory rape, and all the details. Just like Radcliff said. He decides his new plan is not going to work out. Horney old bastard gets an offer for sex from a drugged-out hot chick that doesn't look her age... it's just not the hardcore evil Aidan hoped for. Half the men alive would fall for it. He decides to let him go. His wonderful new plan sucks.

Aidan, lost in thought and staring at the floor, hands the paper back to Radcliff who takes it with his left hand as he raises a revolver from the drawer with his right. Aidan never sees it. Radcliff fires one shot into Aidan's chest.

"OUCH!" he cries and looks down. Angry now, he knocks the gun out of Radcliff's hand. "I was going to let you live, *you jackass.*"

Radcliff's eyes get big again. "What the... *why ain't you dead?*"

Aidan examines the hole from the bullet and the black stains from the gunpowder and is very upset. *"You've ruined me only blazer!"*

Radcliff is too dumbfounded to speak, staring with his mouth open and those buggy eyeballs.

He seizes him by the hair. "You're too dumb to live." Aidan feeds after all.

A few days later the brothers have another heart-to-heart. Liam agrees to enjoy his big brother's hospitality on an open-ended basis, as a thank-you for housing Aidan in Dublin. Liam shops to get furnishings to convert one of the empty rooms into a bedroom. Aidan insists on paying for this because he thinks a spare bedroom is a good idea. Aidan even bought Liam a car, without asking, because he knew Liam would have fought him on it. (The money issue has always rumbled between them.) It's a five year-old Jeep. Liam pretends he's a little angry and grudgingly accepts his brother's generosity. "I can sell it when you leave," Aidan reasons. "Just don't fuck it up."

Tomorrow, Liam will offer his services to any local restaurant that will have him. He wants to work while he stays in America. Aidan thinks Liam should just enjoy himself, and even offers him a "stipend" to stay with him and take care of the house until what they feel will be the inevitable Fiona encounter. Nope. Liam wants to earn his keep.

The money issue between the brothers dates from the deaths of their parents in a plane crash about a year ago. Aidan loved his mother more than anything in the world and she him. Her death was the worst thing that ever happened to him and sent him in a spiral of depression so severe that institutionalization was recommended. Aidan refused and gradually recovered from that debilitating grief.

Aidan was also dad's darling and Liam quite the opposite. They fought terribly and Liam brought out the beast in his father. His dad would eventually play what he imagined was his trump card in the effort to bring his younger son to heel: he threatened Liam with exclusion from the family's legacy and its wealth. Liam, in the final confrontation before he ran away at 17 to live in the big city, at last told his father that he would never take a penny from him if he begged him!

So when his parents died, Aidan inherited quite a treasure. He had never known it existed. The family lived such an austere life, yet his father hoarded a fortune.

Aidan wanted to split the legacy with his brother, but Liam would have nothing to do with it. "That money," he explained to his brother, "is poison. If I take a penny of it for my own then the old bastard would have been right about me. I can take care of myself!"

11

After whisking her away to London, the sinful cleric, Father Kevin O'Doul, took Fiona under his wing. He restrained her through the difficult early days when the new ones have no restraints of their own, just a mindless passion to feed. They flew together to that great city, where O'Doul kept a nice apartment.

For the first week, the most maniacal time in a newborn's new life, the priest brought the prey to *her*, in her chambers, not daring to yet let her loose upon the world. He put the depleted corpses in his freezer, to be disposed *en masse* at month's end, when she would decide to return to Ireland.

Fiona calmed down considerably over those weeks, and the pair of them would hunt together the streets and alleys of London. Fiona was a terrific student. Unlike Aidan, she had (and has) no compunction over the nature of her meals—in fact, the younger the better, the purer the more delightful. She happily traded this new knowledge, this new life, for the frequent sex and extravagant affection which she lavished upon her sire, the wicked Kevin O'Doul.

It was all quite false, of course. O'Doul had *raped* her. She had not forgotten this. In her heart she despised him, but she was afraid of his masterful and hypnotic aura, and his formidable powers and animal cunning.

When he judged that she was capable of standing on her own, O'Doul bought her a ticket back home. She pretended she wanted to stay with him and put up quite the convincing fuss, but O'Doul would not be swayed.

As a departing gift, he arranged a portfolio for Fiona to the tune of three million euros. (O'Doul made his fortune on compound interest over the centuries, his clever investments turning his family's small fortune into a vast treasure.) He emphasized that this must seem like an inexhaustible amount of money to Fiona and cautioned her that it was indeed not. He advised her to live frugally, to stay under the radar.

O'Doul explained to Fiona that there were only a few methods that could bring about her demise: her head being separated from her body, a stake through her heart made of wood or silver, or to be consumed by fire. O'Doul explained that protracted exposure to the sun was very uncomfortable but not deadly unless it lasted for many days—and that was a most excruciating death indeed.

At the airport they parted, and Fiona offered a last sweet kiss to O'Doul before he left her on her own. He condescended to accept the kiss, then pressed her away from him gently.

"See that you remain worthy of what I have given you," he warned her. "If I get wind otherwise I'll have to pay you a visit. Remember that I can as easily take your life away as I have given it to you."

She hated him for those words and would never forgive nor forget them.

When she arrived in Ireland Fiona went straight home. Her mother and two brothers were overjoyed to see her, all their worry at last for naught. Her father ignored her and she him.

She refused to see Aidan, and this caused him much confusion and anguish. He had not seen her since he woke, head sore and bloodied, in the churchyard that fateful night. He was overjoyed at the news of her safe return, but she would not see him, saying in a letter that she would come to him in her own good time. This was difficult for Fiona, but she had a plan.

Fiona stayed for almost two weeks but found that living at home was difficult (she would not discuss what had happened to her, she refused all food, slept the day away and was up all night) and feeding was problematic—the population was simply not dense enough to provide a steady supply of blood for her. The murders she was committing was a thing never seen in these peaceful parts in anyone's memory. A general panic was brewing, and Fiona was getting uneasy. She decided to move to Dublin but told no one of her plans.

On the night that she disappeared, she had two important errands to accomplish.

She entered her father's bedroom at 3 a.m. There she woke him by clutching him by the throat to keep him silent as she recited the litany of offenses he had committed against her and her mother through the years and cursed him for the anguish he had caused her beloved Aidan. And when she was finished, she sucked him dry, with great prejudice, and considered her next task.

12

Aidan likes his new job here in Ann Abor, Michigan USA. He teaches piano and theory and has office hours that keep him busy from 10 a.m. to 3 p.m. Monday through Friday. He has a few good students, although most are musically worthless. This is to be expected.

He has made friends with an attractive young colleague, Sylvia, with whom he plays four-hand piano and duets by Mozart and Schubert. He wants to ask her to his home, but it can't be for a meal, since he doesn't 'eat,' nor does he cook very well. That was a job for ma and Liam. But he misses lovemaking and the longer he goes without, the more demanding the urges become.

He has resigned himself to his old feeding methods—criminals and the various lowlife who provoke him. Some nights he drives to Detroit. That will be a fertile spot for a long time.

Liam is working as a short order cook in Ypsilanti at a local diner (he cooked most of the meals at home in Ireland.) The place is ostensibly 'Greek,' but the only Greek involved in the place is the owner, old and infirm, who is never there. He gets along well with everyone and the waitresses like him because he's handsome and fit, has this dreamy Irish brogue, and treats them with affection. The cook he replaced was, as one of the servers put it, "a royal prick."

Liam has already sampled, in record time, the charms of two of the ladies (neither has a problem with that) and one or the other can sometimes be seen with Liam back at the house. (Never both, but Liam can dream…)

Aidan is okay with the situation. Sometimes he plays the piano for them.

13

By the time Fiona had bought her new Jaguar sedan and was ready to leave New York City for Ann Arbor, she had, with the help of her amazing consort Oliver, spent $35,000 on clothing and accessories. And we're not talking gowns and tiaras here—items for which she would have no real-world use—just the best and most cunningly fashionable day-to-day wear that a woman could ever want.

The things he had taught her! Things like professional manicures and pedicures. Who knew? Hair stylists who did such wonderful things! The marvelous world of shoes, shoes, shoes! But makeup? No need. Ever.

Pre-Oliver, she had no idea how to dress herself and with every new realization came even greater embarrassment at her former comical ignorance. *No wonder Dinah laughed at me,* Fiona recalled. *She was right. She was also a first-class bitch and I'm glad I put an end to her.*

But alas, the handsome and courtly Oliver became possessive, even presumptuous with his greater familiarity. He asked way too many questions relating to things like her never eating, her abhorrence of direct sunlight ("Why do we have to shop at night?"), and finally began pressing her about her last night with him on the boat and the death of Dinah. He was drunk when he interrogated her on this last matter, but showed enough of his true self that, after a two-week heavenly fling Fiona knew it was time to put an end to it. It was also, she decided, time to put an end to Oliver.

All her clothes and accessories are now packed away in good, sturdy luggage in the boot of her new sedan, and she is off to trace the same highways as her ungrateful true love. She has learned much in the past few months and believes she is finally worthy of him. She is brand new for him. Her mind reels in dreams about making love to him again.

My Aidan will never hurt me, she feels. *He believes he hates me, but hate is not the opposite of love. Indifference is the opposite of love and Aidan will never be indifferent toward me. Hate is simply love disappointed, but now I will take all his disappointment away. We are the same, Aidan and me. We are destined for one another for eternity. If he can't see this, I will make it clear.* She wipes away a bloody tear. *O, I miss him so.*

14

When Aidan woke from his beating in the churchyard it was the dead of night and there was blood on his face and in his mouth. He sat up and felt the sticky mess of his head wound and as his consciousness returned his head began to pound. Beside him lay the shovel that he bashed the wicked priest with, and then he him. It was all coming back now. Why hadn't the priest been injured from the massive blow that Aidan squarely delivered? Why was Fiona naked? Was she being raped? Where are they? Where is Fiona? He had failed her.

He rose, unsteady, standing in place to get his bearings. He paced slowly about the yard, seeing nothing but grass and graves. Suddenly the back door to the rectory, which was far and to the right of the church from the yard in the rear, opened and the priest emerged. In an instant he was at Aidan's side.

"Where is Fiona?" Aidan barked at the priest's face, fearless. *"Where is she?"*

"She's inside. Sleeping."

"I want to see her," Aidan said and started toward the back porch. The priest spun Aidan about and held him fast by both upper arms. Aidan struggled madly but his endurance was shot. He chanced a swift knee to the priest's groin, but it had no effect whatever. At last he hung loose, dropped his head, and wept.

"Listen to me, boy," Father O'Doul said. "You are alive by the grace of Fiona. Your life means nothing to me. Fiona and I are going away together. Not for long. She may choose to return, or she may wish to start another life in another place. That is not for me to decide.

But what *is* for me to decide, is your fate. *Are you listening to me?"*

Aidan, exhausted and utterly defeated, simply nodded.

"There need be no dissembling. You will tell Fiona's family the simple truth—that the parish priest has kidnapped her and beat you with a shovel for discovering his plan. You will tell the guards the same when they come to investigate."

"They'll find you! You fucking fiend. *They'll find you!* And if you hurt her I'll.. I'll…"

"You can do *nothing*, you pup. They will *not* find me. Nor will you. She may return and she may not. Those are the truths here."

Aidan looked up into O'Doul's black eyes. "What kind of priest *are* you?"

O'Doul laughed. "The temporary kind," he said. "I find it to be a respite, an occasional retreat from a very busy and very long life. Now it's on to a new chapter."

The priest released Aidan's arms and clutched a wad of his brown hair, yanking him across the grass to where the shovel lay. O'Doul reached down, snatched up the shovel, and gave Aidan an identical bash on the other side of his head. He dropped like a doll.

The next day, Aidan brought the news of the kidnapping to Fiona's family—a tearful and heartbreaking scene. The guards came and questioned Aidan relentlessly. The only thing he held back was Fiona's nakedness and presumed rape. He didn't see why anyone else needed to know about that.

A month went by with no news. Aidan had never in his 20 years felt as much grief and anxiety as he did in those wretched days with his parents dead and Fiona gone. With Liam gone to Dublin more than a year now, Aidan lived alone in the big family home and the solitude had become almost unbearable. The only thing that was worse was the company of others. He craved seclusion but the walls were closing in.

With news of Fiona's return, Aidan's heart nearly exploded with joy and relief. His prayers were answered, and life flooded back into his empty soul. But the joy was not unalloyed, for she refused to see him, telling him in a terse note that she would come to him in the fullness of time.

15

It's a cool night in Ann Arbor and Liam has just arrived home from work and a few drinks afterwards. It's about 10 p.m. He hears piano music as he steps to the front door and waits. Something doesn't sound familiar. *Sounds like more than two hands at work in there*, he thinks, and pushes in.

Sure enough he spies his brother sitting on the bench and a lovely young woman to his right. He's playing low, she's playing the high part. They sound great. Like pros. He stands in the foyer and listens till the movement ends. They stop, smile at one another, and turn to look at Liam.

"Mozart?" Liam guesses.

"Good guess!" chirps the pretty lady.

He gives her a dark look. "Careful of my brother!" Liam warns her falsely. "He's a terrible cad!"

She leans over and kisses Aidan on the cheek. "He is *not!*"

The three share a laugh and Liam storms in, directly to the refrigerator.

"Aidan!" he calls. "There's no beer! Why is this?"

"Probably because you drank it all. We have white wine and vodka. Both cold."

"Vodka it is!" he calls back. "White wine is the decaf of the wine world."

Aidan looks at Sylvia and smiles. "Want a glass of wine? I'm gonna make a drink."

"Yes," she says. "A glass of decaf, if you please." Aidan hops up and heads kitchenward.

"Wow. She's too hot for you," Liam whispers as he pours vodka into two martini glasses. "What's her name?"

"Sylvia. Be nice."

Aidan pours the wine. Liam adds a touch of vermouth to the vodka. "Where are the olives. Get the olives."

Aidan does as requested. "No olive for me."

"You'll have an olive and like it."

"Aye, will I indeed?"

"You will." Liam unscrews the bottle and puts on a solemn face. "The martini garnish is the only thing that separates us from the animals. You don't actually have to eat it."

"You know what you can do with that olive?"

Liam reaches into Aidan's glass, fishes out the olive and drops it into his own with a plunk. Now he has two.

"You're not gonna eat *her,* are you?" Liam whispers.

"Not like you think. And shut up."

Liam vulgarly licks his lips and gives his brother a gooney grin.

They repair to the living room. Sylvia has relocated to a couch, all snuggled in with a blanket over her. Aidan sits in the middle, close to her. Liam takes a La-Z-Boy. They chat for a while, get to know one another, but not too long. Liam is not boorish enough to impede an obvious romance in the offing. He soon heads off to his room, and to sleep.

The two lovebirds cuddle up close and make out, all very chaste, "like high schoolers," Sylvia remarks. Aidan wonders if that's a hint that he's dawdling when the girl wants to zoom. He invites her into his bedroom, and she accepts the invitation with grace and a smile.

16

After leveling the score by feeding upon her louse of a father and leaving her family home in the Irish outback for the last time, Fiona turned to her second task of the night. She would finally visit the solitary Aidan in his big house over the hill.

It was almost 4 a.m. when she knocked on the great wooden door of the Bell home. Bleary Aidan opened the door, gasped and bear-hugged Fiona as tightly as he could, burying his head into her neck and heaving great sighs. She allowed this, joyously, and waited patiently until he at last released her. He took her hand and pulled her inside, shutting the door.

"Jaysus, your hand is cold."

"It's a cool night," Fiona said. "I walked."

"Where have you been, love? All this time."

"Six weeks."

"You say it like it's no big deal! My god, we were dyin' here! Me. Your ma, Davie and Mike." He collected himself. "I'm sorry. Jeez. Would you like a drink?"

"Maybe a glass of gin? With ice?"

He frowned. "No gin. Whisky?"

She smiled a big yes and he's off to pour two drinks.

She sat on a sofa, making room for Aidan next to her. He entered with the drinks and handed Fiona a glass. She belted it back in a single draught and handed the glass back to Aidan, who laughed.

"Thirsty, are we?"

"Let's just say 'dry.'"

"So," Aidan said, settling in. "Tell."

Fiona smiled and asked, "How do I look?"

Aidan was confused. "How do you look? You look like you've come back!"

For a moment Fiona thought that all of her efforts to be the best she could be were for naught, lost on her dear bumpkin love. But then it opened to her like a glorious moonrise—*he loves me for me, not my clothes or my new sophistication or my perfected beauty. It's me he loves.* And with this realization she loved him in that moment more than she had ever loved anything in her life. She was right to come to him. He is the one. He always was. She teared up, but they were tears of blood. Wiping them away quickly, she stood and then kneeled in front of Aidan and put her head in his lap.

"Aidan my darling. I have loved you all my life. And I have something to ask you."

"Aye. Whatever it is. You only need to ask."

She lifted her head and met the eyes of her true love. He was smiling.

"Will you make love to me? It seems I've been waiting all my life… for that." She paused. "Have you never wanted to have me that way, Aidan?"

"Well… I'd be lying if I said that I didn't. I mean… I'm a human male," he laughed. "And you… you are…"

She moved close to his face. "Say it."

He looked at her now as if seeing her for the first time. As if in a daze.

"You are… more lovely that ever you were."

That was a kissing cue if she ever heard one, and so they did.

In their afterglow, Fiona put her head on Aidan's bare chest as they lay in his bed.

He stroked her hair, and as he did she whispered, "You are the sweetest, gentlest most perfect lover any woman could ever want." This was no silly love-talk; she meant it, from the bottom of her heart. In retrospect, this would become the highlight of her life, the old life and the new—she had achieved a perfect peace and the acme of her ambition. To experience it again would be the propellant that would drive her every action and obsess her completely.

"And you're perfect," he said, as if a little surprised. "I mean…"

"What? Say it."

"Well… didn't you have that wee twist in your spine? It was hardly noticeable, but… your wutchacallit?"

"My scoliosis."

"Yeah. That."

"It went away."

"And the nail on your little finger that you lost when we were, what, eight? When that thing happened?"

"It grew back." He traced a line on her hip. "And yes," she said, "that scar is gone now."

"Wow."

They just lay there, basking in the loveglow for a quiet space and then Aidan could hold back no longer.

"Can we talk about… the thing with the priest? That night?"

"Yes. But first I have a gift for you."

Aidan laughed. "You do? I like gifts. What is it?"

Fiona lifted her head and scooted up a little. They were nose-to-nose.

"Perfection," she said.

"Really! Well then. Let's have it!"

17

When Liam ran away from his home and family, bitterly rejecting his father's legacy and a fortune the extent of which he had little idea, he made a beeline to Dublin, hitching rides all the way. He arrived in the big city about 1 p.m. with €55 to his name. (For puzzled Americans, that's a little over $60.) Hardly a nestegg.

A poor student with few saleable skills and little ambition, Liam found himself alone and afraid. After an afternoon spent wandering the city getting the lay of the land, he drifted to the outskirts a bit apart from the hustle and bustle. The sun was setting, and he was feeling blue, so naturally, he looked for a pub.

As he walked past an unassuming corner establishment dubbed *The Vessel,* he felt a strong pull toward the door. There was a menu taped to the inside of the window. Liam studied it hungrily. Typical pub fare with nothing standing out as special, he was nevertheless so famished from his busy food-free day that the menu seemed to Liam as a litany of one princely delight after another. He entered, wiping saliva from his chin.

As pubs go it was medium-sized, bar along the wall, maybe 15 tables, 2- and 4-tops and a big table in the far corner with eight stools. This was across from a raised bandstand, empty now (it was just past 7 p.m.) but he noted a gaggle of obvious musicians (or possibly vagrants) at a nearby table. Nice wood everywhere, especially the bar itself, which gleamed with a proud polish.

Liam took a seat at the bar and surveyed the clientele—three pair of men at tables, three women at another, and an ancient gentleman at the other end of the bar. Behind the bar was an incredibly wide fellow with a ready smile.

"What'll it be, mate?"

Liam spun on his stool and said loudly, "A round for everyone!"

His generosity was happily acknowledged by all, the geezer at the bar raising his Guinness glass to Liam.

"And for you?" the barman asked.

"Guinness. Please." Liam held out his hand. "I'm Liam."

"Dillon," the barman said and shook Liam's hand, and with a smile turned and commenced his sacred duty.

As Liam finished his first beer, another automagically appeared to take its place, courtesy of that wonderful pub tradition that would oblige the others to keep 'em comin', at least for a few more rounds. Before Dillon moved on, Liam asked if he might sample from the menu. Dillon darkened and gestured toward the door that led to the kitchen.

"My 'chef,' as he likes to be called, is in his last week here. So he's hammered. And I don't trust him right now to boil water in a pan."

"Ah…" Liam replied. "I was hoping for coddle and maybe some champ to go with. Possible?"

Dillon looked embarrassed. "'Tis been a bad week…"

"How about this," Liam suggested. "I'll go back and make it."

"You?" Dillon was a little skeptical.

"Aye. I can make everything on your menu," Liam said. "And you'll never taste boxty like me own."

Dillon just stared at him, for a hard ten seconds, then said, "You just need to heat up the coddle, it's good from last night, but you'll have to make the champ. I might be crazy but… Come with me. I'll give you a little tour of the back."

He never asked Liam about his experience, knowing through hard experience of his own that it only matters what you can actually *do*, not what you claim, with a reasonable amount of reliability thrown in. He wanted to see if Liam could walk his talk. What the hell—there was nothing to lose.

The coddle looked okay to Liam. It was a bacon, sausage, potatoes, and onions affair stewed in layers.

"For a customer I'd put it in a covered pan with a little water and steam it hot," Liam explained. "But I'm hungry so I'll just nuke it."

Dillon nodded and glanced over at his 'chef' who had fallen from his chair and was snoring loudly on the kitchen floor. Dillon shook his head in disgust.

Liam snatched up a chef's knife and tested the edge with his thumb.

"Jesus, Dillon. Is there a honing stick in the house? I've used butter knives with a keener edge."

Dillon fetched the honing stick and swore loudly. "I don't know what happened to the lazy bastard! He used to be a decent cook. Fuck all. A pub kitchen with dull knives."

Liam worked the knife deftly against the ceramic wand, shaking his head. "Dillon, these things need *sharpening*. A honing won't do. It's gone beyond."

"It'll have to do tonight," Dillon said.

Putting a slightly better edge on the blade, Liam took the cold baked potato that Dillon offered him, skinned and chopped it in a wink, diced some green onions with TV-chef-showing-off facility and put all in a pan. He heated it up with some butter and milk, and at the right time began to expertly mash the potatoes till all was smooth and creamy. He plated the dish, salted and peppered nicely, and garnished with the sliced green part of the onion.

"When 'chef' here makes it, it's a little gluey," Dillon said glumly.

"That's because he over-mashes the potatoes." He looked over at the sleeping drunk. "Like a monkey might."

"And no garnish. Ever," Dillon mourned. "On anything."

Liam gave Dillon a soulful look, putting a hand on the big man's shoulder. "The garnish, my friend, is the only thing that separates us from the animals."

Dillon glanced over at his plastered 'chef.' "When I look at that creature I am inclined to believe you."

As if on cue, the drunk man awoke and rose unsteadily, stood tall and tried to look important.

"What in hell is *he* doin' here?" 'Chef' asked. He was tall and skinny, looked about 60, five-day beard, ragged.

"He's my new cook." He looked quickly over to Liam and raised his eyebrows. Liam smiled and nodded assent. "Yes. My new cook. Now fuck off out of here and don't come back."

"But I'm here till-"

"I'll pay you to stay home for the week. Now piss off!" 'Chef' stormed through the kitchen door muttering curses and filthy oaths.

Liam nuked his coddle while the champ cooled a bit, and Dillon invited him to sit at the kitchen table and enjoy his meal while Dillon cared for the customers who were feeling abandoned. When he finished, he offered to start work immediately, an offer Dillon gladly accepted. It was a blessedly slow night that allowed Liam to become familiar with the equipment and the location of everything. The only thing that truly intimidated him was the big fryer—he had never used one. Dillon would tutor him and eventually show him how to keep stock and make orders, things all new to Liam but essential for a commercial enterprise.

There was music every night at *The Vessel,* but Monday night was a simple affair that sorted with the smaller crowd and featured a young lady who played the guitar and sang. Her name was Veronica. She was homely in a sweet way, thin and vulnerable-looking with straight black hair and big eyes.

Friday night at *The Vessel*

Liam took a break during her first set and sat at the bar to listen to her play. She was at her best at the forlorn ballad, the Irish repertory supplying plenty of those, but most of the pub musicians played pop hits mixed in aplenty, and so did she. Her innocence and vulnerability bewitched him, and he felt protective of her.

It was after midnight and Veronica was finishing her final set. The kitchen was closed, and Liam sat at

'Dillon's table' with the boss. They felt joyous inside. Dillon was pleased that Liam might actually work out, and of course, Liam had a job! The details were still fuzzy—nonexistent, actually—but Liam had faith in the process.

There were only a few customers, most solitary and at different tables. The door opened and another shuffled in, taking a place at the bar. Dillon rose and took his order, which was for beer, which is Irish for Guinness. The man was already drunk and not a regular, judging by Dillon's terse exchange with the man.

Dillon resumed his seat with his new cook and asked Liam where he lived. Liam said nowhere.

"I just got to town. I ran away from me da. I have, I dunno, €10 to my name and I thank you and God for my new job. I won't let you down."

Dillon considered this. He was both astonished and impressed at the honestly of the lad, the sincerity. Dillon had always prided himself as a good judge of men (Women? Not so much.) and, except for 'chef' he's had few regrets on that score over the years. He had a good feeling about Liam and resolved to help him.

"Come with me," he said.

There was one other door behind the bar, and it was the entrance to Dillon's 'office.' A desk with a laptop PC, chair, lamp, file cabinet, printer, barstool and army cot. That and a few pics on the wall of various family members. Dillon unlocked the door and gave Liam a peek inside.

"Welcome to your new home. We'll see how things work out this week, and if we get on, I'll make you a key. You sleep here, but no food in here, if you please. After a few paychecks you'll have some place of your own. What do you say?"

Liam, to his own surprise, started to tear up. Dillon was uncomfortable with this.

"Hey now! Buck up, lad," he said.

Liam wiped at his face. "I'm sorry. It's just that…" He couldn't finish the sentence.

"Let's go back and have a wee dram of Redbreast and toast our good fortune."

That snapped Liam out of it enough to smile and simply say thanks.

They noted once they sat, with their two small glasses of Redbreast before them, that the man at the bar had placed himself on a stool at the foot of the bandstand directly in front of Veronica. She was singing an old ABBA song, *Dancing Queen*. She was halfway through when the man in front of her yelled for her to stop. She did.

"What's wrong?" she asked timidly.

"Don't sing that shite, you're no good at it!" he slurred loudly. Veronica put her hand to her mouth and her eyes got really big. "Sing another sad thing. You're good at them. Better anyway."

Veronica looked as though she was about to burst into tears.

He's right, Liam thought. *But not like that.* He bolted from his seat and rushed the man, who stood up to face him. Liam punched the fellow in his well-muscled gut, and he doubled over. He spun the man about, seized him by the back of his collar and his belt and shouted to Dillon.

"Open the door!"

Dillon complied as Liam administered a textbook 'bum's rush' out the door, and onto the sidewalk the rude fellow tumbled. It would have been a '10' in the Bar Bouncer Olympics. They both watched as the fellow struggled to stand, moaning. He gave them the finger and stumbled on his way.

"*I never paid my tab, arseholes!*" was his parting shot.

"Take it out of my pay," Liam said to Dillon as he closed the door.

"Not on your life, lad," Dillon said, but he looked worried. Liam asked what was the matter. "Well... I'm not sure if I regret it now that I've hired you... or if I'm even happier about it now than I *was!*"

Liam clapped him on the shoulder. "We'll work it out!"

They turned and Veronica blocked their way. She held out her hand to Liam.

"I'm Veronica. We've not been introduced. You can call me Ronnie."

"Oh!" Liam a little flustered. He pumped her hand. "I'm Liam. Umm... call me *that.*" He let go her hand.

"No one has ever done anything that nice for me in my whole life."

"Well... we can't let that sort of thing go on. In a nice place. Like this. To a nice girl. Like-"

Before he finished his lame stammer she leaned up and kissed him on the cheek. She smiled at his blush and headed back to the stage.

"That's enough, Ronnie," Dillon said. "Go home, darlin'. It's been a long day."

One of the few remaining patrons objected. "Hey! We come late to see her specially!"

Liam turned and looked hard at the fellow.

"Never mind," the man said.

18

The killing spree that Aidan and Fiona sparked rocked the nation of Ireland. Investigations concluded that there were 20 murders attributed to a pair of serial killers working as a team in a three-week period, all in widespread rural areas or villages centered about 160 kilometers northwest of Dublin. This much the authorities knew.

They did not know if the many others reported missing during this time, mostly children, were connected to the pair, but confidence was high. 'Exsanguination,' *to deprive of or drain of blood,* was the assigned cause of death in every case. Attendant trauma, which could not be contained from press reports, was without exception: *two puncture wounds in the neck.*

The press went wild with this, of course, theorizing wildly while the authorities struggled to keep a general calm while withholding as many of the worst details of the cases as they could manage, with little success on both counts. The more reasonable people thought it to be a clever duo creating the illusion of vampire activity to enhance the horror element of their deeds; a sizeable minority believed it was the real thing.

It was all Fiona could do to keep Aidan under any measure of control during those weeks. (It gave her some indication of how she must have taxed her sire, the priest O'Doul, during her days as a neophyte.) Aidan was stronger than Fiona, and her attempts at physical restraint were often ineffective.

The first week was the hardest, and there were many close calls in their attempts to feed. There was no caution, let alone finesse, in Aidan's search for blood. They would hunt as a pair, with Aidan promising to do Fiona's bidding and behave with some caution when, for example, they would come upon a farmhouse and Aidan would suddenly sprint away so fast that only eyes like Fiona's could see him in his flight. He would snatch a child from her sandbox, and sprint ahead of Fiona. Aidan would be feeding voluptuously by the time she would catch up with him. That they were never observed in the act was an uncanny bit of luck.

The second week was easier, and by the middle of the third week Aidan felt as though he had suddenly come to his senses. Too suddenly, as in, without warning. Unlike Fiona, he was experiencing a deepening dissatisfaction with all that had transpired, but at first it was just a general feeling, the fog gradually clearing.

Aidan Bell's family home in Ireland

At dusk, Aidan rose from a most troubled sleep. He sought out Fiona in her room in Aidan's house where they had passed the weeks of carnage. She was sleeping. He sat in a chair next to her bed and waited until she woke. As she slept he studied her perfect face. *What did she do to me?* He wondered. *How could she have done this to me?*

Certainly, he rejoiced in his new skills, in the restoration of all his minor but various physical imperfections. He gloried in his speed, strength, reflexes, stamina, his incredibly enhanced sensorium, as well as the perfect confidence that all this lent. Who would not? But this was *physical*. What troubled Aidan went far beyond.

At last Fiona opened her eyes, saw Aidan, and smiled. Her face darkened as she sensed his distemper.

"What's wrong?" she whispered.

"What did you do to me?" he asked, as if in a trance. "Is this what the priest did to you? And now you've done it to me?"

"I see you've… recovered." She was looking forward to this time, to their renewed lovemaking, when the quest for fresh blood would not be Aidan's only passion, but her expectations were falling short. How short?

"I suppose I have-," and he stopped, and a look of terror changed his face. He stood and gasped, frozen in fear.

"What's wrong, Aidan? Why-"

"I'm a murderer! I've drained screaming, terrified children of their blood! I've murdered babies for my food! What have you done!?!?"

"Aidan, everything is different now, you see-"

"I've murdered innocent people! I held them close and felt their terror as I sucked the lifeblood from their bodies! AND I REJOICED IN THIS! Mothers, fathers… toddlers! WHAT

82

HAVE YOU DONE TO ME?" he was screaming at her at the top of his lungs as his memories flooded unbidden into consciousness.

"Aidan, until you calm down nothing will make sen-"

"And when I'm calm I'll understand why I've become a fucking monster? And that will be okay? What's happened to me? What's happened to you?!"

"We've become-"

"I'll never see the sun again! The food I used to eat disgusts me! I'll need blood, blood, BLOOD! My life is over!" he wailed.

"Aidan, your life is just beg-"

He got all icy cold and calm all of a sudden and whispered, "You absolute fucking horror of a woman."

Fiona was shocked. "Aidan, you don't mean that."

"You've sent me to hell," he seethed.

"I've made you immortal," she said.

He stared at her hard, as if he had never seen her before, and indeed, he had not.

"You had no choice in what was done to you," he said, less frosty now. "There is some redemption there. But you *did* have a choice to make me like he made you."

"But life without you… Aidan… I couldn't bear it. I wanted to make you as I am. Immortal. Strong! New!"

"Get out."

Did she hear that right? "What?"

"Get the fuck out of my house. You made me like you because you're a selfish, deranged… *horror* of a woman. Get out or I will throw you out the window."

Sensing the truth in his threat, and as if in a daze, Fiona rose, quickly dressed, and gathered her few personal effects. Aidan ushered her to the door where she turned and said, "You will love me again."

"I will nev-"

"When you discover who you really are, you will love me again. You will become grateful for all I have done for you. And for us." She wiped away a bloody tear, gazed up at him and whispered passionately, "I promise you: *I will live only for this. Only for us.*"

When she had finally loaded up the boot of her leased Volvo and sped away, Aidan felt lost in guilt and shame. He resolved to sell his home, furnishings included. He resolved to walk away from all he had held dear for his entire life. He would gather a few effects from the house, and drive to Dublin to see his brother and spill his heart to him.

19

Sylvia sits naked on the edge of Aidan's bed, her feet on the floor. Her head is turned away from Aidan who sits next to her, brushing her long brown hair. It has only been a few weeks, but Aidan is in love with her, and she with him. He feels that she is the one and he has to tell her about whom and what he is. He stops brushing, leans and kisses her shoulder. Sylvia turns and throws her arms around Aidan, pushing her breasts against his chest.

"Mmmmm… let's make love!" Sylvia suggests gaily.

"I need to talk to you," he says.

"Really? Now?" This is not like him.

"Yeah, now," he says. "But not here. Let's go for a ride."

"This late? I thought we were going to *sleep!* It's almost 10 o'clock."

"Indulge me."

She considers this briefly. "Your car?"

"No. The bike. Not many riding nights left."

"Where to?"

"The woods. Some public land west of here."

This baffles and mystifies Sylvia. But she'll go along. She wants to be with him.

They dress and are out the door in minutes, and it *is* a lovely night. A little muggy but in the mid-70s, the sky clear, and as they cruise their way down Dexter Road the stars multiply away from the city lights. Sylvia holds on tight to her man.

It takes about 20 minutes for Aidan to get to the Pinckney Recreation Area, a vast stretch of wooded land with lots of lakes and streams and beautiful scenic roads and trails. The obscure dirt road he's on has been recently groomed and a pleasure to mosey down at low speed. He spots the trail into the woods he was hunting for and turns off the road, venturing in about 50 yards. He stops and shuts the bike off.

"Listen!" he whispers. A minute passes.

"I don't hear anything," Sylvia says.

"I know. Right?"

She laughs. "Yes. It *is* quiet here. And did you see the stars on the way down the road? We don't get them much at home do we?"

They dismount the big Beemer and Sylvia stretches her lean body.

"Ah! That feels good!' she says.

"Is there anything you want to ask me?" Aidan says, abruptly.

"Wait, what? I thought you wanted to show me something."

"I do, but... you must have some questions. Noticed a few things about me these past few weeks."

She rests her butt on the bike's seat and ponders a space.

"Well... I never see you *eat*... for one thing. Like... *ever!*"

Aidan looks at the ground and nods. The near-full moon brightens the scene enough for Sylvia to see.

She's uncomfortable with where this is headed. "Do we really need to do this?"

"I think we do. Yes. Anything else?"

"Well... you're perfectly beautiful."

"Thanks," he laughs. "So are you."

"Hardly, but thanks."

"What else?"

"Your body is..."

"What? Say it."

"Kind of cold. Like... not unpleasant or anything, just... not warm. That's a little odd I guess."

"Go on."

"Okay. The big thing. My only complaint, really... is that we never go out in the daytime! Never just enjoy the sunshine together. Not even at the college. You never go on walks with me there. It's like you're..."

"Like I'm what?"

"Like you're afraid."

"Got it. Go on."

"That's about it. Except... what are you doing here?"

"Wha... what do you mean?"

"You're *way* too good a pianist to be at Concordia. I *never* saw a technique like you have. You're a virtuoso's virtuoso. Like the rumors about Michelangeli—I've never once seen or heard you play a wrong note. You should be, like, historically famous. And your memory is the best! And your sight-reading... it's better than the studied performances I know from *recordings*. You're actually a little... I don't know... *discouraging*. I mean... I know I'm good. I placed second in Warsaw, for god's sake. But *you?* You're as far from me as I am from a rank beginner."

"I can explain all this," he is quick to say.

"Okay. Then... please do," she says, a little dejectedly.

He sighs. He thought he knew how to do this, rehearsing it all constantly, but he's forgotten it all and what he recalls seems inept now. The real reason for his silence suddenly and rudely occurs to him.

"I'm afraid if I tell you I'll lose you," he blurts, and covers his face with his hands.

She rushes to him and holds him tight.

"No, no, no, no, no. That could never, *ever* happen." She comforts him as if he were a child. He presses her to him. "Don't be afraid to tell me the truth," she says, and they stand apart.

"I'm what…" he struggles mightily. "I'm what people call… a vampire."

Sylvia smiles. "Go on. Tell me more."

Okay, that was an interesting response. Aidan considers how to advance the situation. He looks about and selects a nearby tree, about eight inches in diameter.

"Watch this, Sylvia," he says. Aidan places his left palm on the back of the tree and with the heel of his right hand he strikes the front of the tree a few inches above where his other hand has braced. With a sound like a shotgun blast the tree snaps in two, the tall tree flipping in the air and landing sideways a few feet in front of them. The bang still echoes.

Sylvia's eyes grow large at the demonstration, her jaw open. Aidan reaches down and picks up a rock, about the size of an elongated coconut. He squeezes both ends toward the center and the rock explodes into crumbles. He looks at Silvis to note the effect and sees that she is standing firm and not in a panic.

Now he calls to her and she looks about, not seeing him.

"Up here, Sylvia," he calls again.

Aidan is sitting in a tree a few yards away, at least 50 feet above her. She spies him. That's his cue to jump and land safely on his feet. He trods over to her.

"Don't be afraid," he says. He offers her his hand, but she freezes. He understands. She stands stock still with glazed eyes at Aidan. He waits.

"How can I not be afraid?" she says in an unsteady voice. "How can you do these things?"

"There's more. I got shot in the chest a couple weeks ago and all it did was hurt. And piss me off. You see, I only have the one blazer, and I-"

"Blazer?! What the hell are you talking about?"

"I DON'T KNOW!"

"Don't yell!... Please."

"Fuck all to hell, I dunno," he mumbles and turns away from her, rubbing his forehead. "That's not the main thing, though," he says. How can he possibly tell her about *the main thing?*

"So, the sunlight," she says quietly, regaining her composure enough to converse. Aidan turns to face her.

"Yeah. The sun," he explains monotonously. "Umm… I can't go out in the sun or it'll kill me. Incredibly painful. So I have to avoid the sun. When I ride to work I have full-body coverage and a helmet with a full mask sunshield. I dread the winter because I don't know how I can outfit the car to protect me."

Her natural terror is alloyed by his vulnerability and willingness to bare all to her. She knows it must be terribly hard.

She walks to him and puts her arms around his neck. He embraces her.

"Who else knows?" she asks.

"My brother. And one other."

"The one who made you like this?"

"Yes." He pushes her away. "But the sunlight. That's not the main thing."

She thinks, and suddenly puts her hand to her mouth. "O no! It's why you don't eat. It's about that, isn't it?" She backs away. "O no, Aidan, *no.*"

Does Sylvia think she is in danger? He almost laughs.

"Sylvia, darlin'… where are you going!" She makes a run for it down the trail, but Aidan is at the road waiting for

her. He holds her firmly by her upper arms. She's immobile.

"I'll scream!"

"Why?" he asks calmly. She looks confused.

"Why did you take me all the way out here?" she demands.

"For a demonstration," he smiles. "That's all. How could you think I could ever hurt you?" He can feel her relax and he releases her. She rubs her arms.

"I'm sorry, Aidan," she says quietly. "I panicked. I'm okay now." She looks at him as if she's never seen him before. "But you need to explain."

He can't look at her while he says the words.

"I need human blood to live."

Big sigh from Sylvia. "How do you get it?"

"From criminal, thugs, lowlifes who attack me. I never initiate it."

"Why do they attack you?" Aiden feels like he's a boy in the confessional.

"Because I provoke them with my presence."

"Explain this, please."

"I go where I'm not welcome."

"Such as?"

"Neighborhoods. Certain bars and clubs. Or sometimes I'll read about someone released from jail who I think ought to still be there. Or else should never have made it there in the first place. Once I tried to limit my diet to sex offenders, but some of them just aren't bad enough for killing, and there's no way to tell what they did before I confront them. So *that* didn't work out too well."

"Why go where you're not welcome?"

Aidan glares at her and seethes. "No one tells me where I can and can't go."

"I see…"

"You see, eh? Hey. You know what? That's enough *unburdening.*" He's growing angry. "I never asked to become this way. Except when I was new, and completely insane for a brief time, I have never harmed an innocent, or fed on someone who has not physically assaulted me or threated me with a weapon. *And that's me. That's who I am. That's who I must be. And you'll have me, or you won't. But I'll be goddamned to fucking hell if I'll apologize for who and what I am!*"

Sylvia cowers away at his rage.

"And now. Unless you want to walk back to Ann Arbor, get your arse back on my bike."

On the ride back to town, at full speed, scaring the hell out of the poor girl, Aidan is glad he isn't in the car because he doesn't want to talk. But he does want to think. He drives straight to Sylvia's house in the middle of town and stops the bike. She dismounts, steps up and embraces Aidan about the neck. He hesitates only slightly before he hugs her to himself. They remain like this for a space. She pulls away and kisses his cheek.

She smiles as if nothing's happened. "I don't want to go home. Take me back and love me in your bed." In what is meant to be a humorous gesture, Aidan revs up his bike loudly. VROOM-VROOM! He sees it's lost on her, and he simply nods and returns her smile. She hops back on.

And off they go.

20

By the evening after the day that Aidan threw Fiona out of his ancestral home, Aidan had gathered together the few things he wanted to take with him into this new life that the selfish vixen had thrust upon him.

He had opted not to sell the house; it might one day be a handy retreat and the money was not an issue. He had an old Toyota on its last legs, a small car with a boot that just managed to contain the few things that he took from home. As soon as it was dark, he said goodbye to his house and hills and started the drive to Dublin.

He arrived at the city limits well before midnight and drove straight to *The Vessel*, as Liam had instructed him to do by phone that afternoon. He parked in a dark part of the lot, sat in the car, and considered his situation. He had to feed. The hunger was no longer a blinding and insanely passionate craving as it was in previous weeks, but it was bad enough to know he couldn't put it off much longer. He had to be choosy now, avoid the innocent. He had no idea how to proceed.

He knew he could live with Liam at his new flat and was welcome there until he found a place of his own, and he was so close to his classes and duties at Trinity College that he could get there by Dublin Bus in minutes, although the helmet and full-body sun protection he had to wear was as bizarre as it was uncomfortable. (When he was a younger he would drive for hours three times a week for lessons from his home, because his father would not pay for his board at Trinity, citing the uselessness of a career in music.)

His car was on its last legs. Or wheels. Aidan could smell steam from the radiator. He would need to address that quickly. With his new riches, the world of wheels was wide open to him.

But first on his list was a reunion with his dear brother whom he had rarely seen in more than a year other than the odd lunch between classes and a stop at *The Vessel* now and again for a quick pint. He hopped out of the smelly car and made his way into the pub.

"Aye, Liam! You said he was comin' and there's himself now!" cried Wee Dillon from behind the bar, loud enough for Liam to hear in the kitchen.

In seconds Liam emerged, wiping hands on a towel as he made his way to his brother. He threw the towel over his shoulder and the brothers embraced.

"Welcome to Dublin, Aidan," Liam said, releasing him. "It's good to see you."

"And you, Liam."

Dillon was next in line for a hug. "Aye, Aidan. Good to see you. Are you hungry? No? Thirsty then."

"Maybe a nice vodka martini?"

"Or two!" shouted Dillon as he hurried back to fulfill the request.

They headed to 'Dillon's table,' and Aidan looked about. The place was half-full, and a gaggle of musicians were preparing for their last set of the night. He sat.

Liam wouldn't sit. "Bollocks! I need to cook," he said, annoyed.

"Plenty of time, brother. You'll be sick of me in no time."

"You're daft. I'm glad to have you!" And Liam headed back to his domain in the kitchen.

Dillon appeared with Aidan's first martini of the night. "Listen. Ronnie will take care of you." He pointed. "That's her taking an order in the back, see? I told her to treat you right." And at that Dillon went back to tend the busy bar. Aidan was content just to sit and drink.

The door opened and a large man in full leathers carrying a helmet made his way in and sat at a corner table, his back to the wall. He looked like a tough-guy, or what Aidan thought a tough-guy would look before his change. Tough-guy sat a moment, stood, took off his jacket and draped it over an adjacent chair. He then stepped to the end of the bar and waved Dillon over.

Dillon looked uncomfortable with the short conversation. The biker muscled Dillon aside and entered the kitchen. Aidan stood, uneasy, and Dillon rushed from behind the bar to confront Aidan, sensing danger.

"Better just stay here, Aidan. It'll be okay."

Aidan sensed differently. "Who's the chancer?"

Dillon hunted for the words. "He's a collector."

"Jesus, don't tell me…"

"Liam owes money. And it's more than I can front him. He comes every week, more like every other night now. But Liam says he has a plan. He's working it out with him."

"Maybe I can help." Aidan pushed past Dillon and headed behind the bar, carefully opening the kitchen door and entering. Liam and Tough-guy stood facing one another, and they both looked to Aidan as he entered, and closed the door behind him.

"Get lost," Tough-guy gruffed.

"Liam," Aidan said calmly. "What's going on here."

Tough-guy turned to Liam. "Get him out of here."

"Shut your hole. I'm not going anywhere."

"Maybe you better, Aidan," Liam said. "I can handle this. We'll talk later."

Tough-guy stepped toward Aidan. "Did you just tell me to 'shut my ho-'"

Aidan lashed out with a punch to the man's head that was so fast that Liam did not see it happen. He just saw Tough-guy fall backwards to the floor.

"Jesus, did you…" Liam stuttered. "Did… what did you do?"

"I hit him. He's out for now. What's going on, Liam. Why do you owe this guy?"

"Okay…" Liam stammered, gesturing with his hands that everything was fine, just fine. "I used to be heavy into opioids. Not anymore, though. Not for months. Almost lost my job. Borrowed money from Dillon." Whispering now. "I even stole from him, but he doesn't know."

"How much are you in for?"

"Three thousand euros and… and some change."

Aidan did some quick thinking. "Listen to me, Liam, and don't even try to stop what I have in mind here. It'll be okay. I can pay that off-"

"I'll pay you back!"

"Yes, I know. God forbid you accept a money favor from me. But stay out of my hair for a half-hour. Promise?"

"What will you do?"

"God damn it! Promise me right now you'll stay in the kitchen here and do your work until I return. Promise!"

Liam sighed. "Okay. I promise."

Aidan grabbed Tough-guy by his long filthy hair and dragged him through the back door of the kitchen into the dark yard. He found a likely spot and bent over the body, feeding voluptuously. When he was at last sated he checked the now-dead man's clothing and found just a wallet with nothing of interest inside apart from a few hundred euros, which he kept. He hefted the corpse, waited till the coast was clear, then carried the body to his car. He opened the back door and threw the body into the back seat. Then he had to empty the boot onto the lot, deftly move the corpse from the back seat to the boot and refill the backseat with the former contents of the boot. Finally, he locked the doors and headed back into the bar.

Once inside he went to the corner table and riffled through the former tough-guy's jacket. He found a set of keys with one sporting a Harley-Davidson logo. He pocketed the keys, and in seconds Liam and Dillon had appeared. Liam said something but Dillon couldn't hear over the din of an Irish reel. Aidan snatched the helmet off the chair, and they stepped outside to talk.

"What happened?" Liam asked.

"I took care of him."

Dillon looked confused. "What does that me-"

"Listen to me. He's gone." Aidan looked at his brother. "Who do you owe the money to?"

"Ah... a dealer in town."

"We'll deliver the money to him personally tomorrow."

Liam fished around in his jean's pocket and pulled out a key.

"This is a key to my place. You've driven by it and you remember where it is, right?"

"I do."

"I'll see you when I get home, okay?"

Liam embraced his brother and a worried-looking Dillon followed. The pair said goodnight and re-entered the pub.

Aidan stepped out back and scouted for the big bike. He spied it at the far end of the lot and made his way to it. He put the helmet on, a little big, and assessed the Harley. It was about a decade old but in fine shape.

Tough-guy had cherished it. Aidan beheld his new set of wheels and grinned. He unlocked the bike, mounted, started it up in a roar, puttered it carefully out of the lot and pulled up to a traffic signal. Aidan delighted in the motorcycle's assertive sound signature. (Keep saying 'potato, potato, potato…' as fast as you can. It sounded just like that.) The light changed and Aidan zoomed his way to Liam's apartment.

21

Her journey nearing its end, Fiona enters the city limits of Ann Arbor at last. She is thoroughly sick of driving. She had easily traced Liam's phone (the eejit!) to a diner in Ypsilanti, the town next door, and then to a house west of town. She spots a Holiday Inn and pulls in. She checks the clock. It's 3 a.m.

Her plan is to unpack, take a shower (though she has become partial to long luxurious bathing, and she may opt for a bath after all) and watch TV before the sun comes up. She has recently fed (a toddler on a porch swing as appetizer, followed by a stout Ohio farmboy whom she tried to seduce first but he was too dim-witted to take advantage of the opportunity), so that won't be a pressing issue.

She gets herself a suite with a jacuzzi and reserves a week in advance. She likes the jacuzzi and makes a note to herself that she'll require one when she has a place of her own. After her ablutions she sprawls in her king-sized bed with the eight pillows comfortably arranged and considers the morrow. She'll drop by Liam's residence after dark and find out from him where Aidan is hiding. (She is unaware that the brothers live together there.)

O Aidan, the poor dear. She knows that he has had much time to consider his new life and what he owes her. He must be glorying in his powers by now, and she is sure that he misses her. Must miss her terribly now that he's had a chance to assess all that has come to pass and all that he has become. And all because of her!

22

Aidan found his brother's flat in that seedy nearby Dublin neighborhood, secured his newly acquired bike, and took the stairs (the lift OUT OF ORDER) to the third floor of the old building to number 311—home sweet home. The place was immaculate. Liam, for all his juvenile delinquent qualities had always been neat. Neat and clean—almost a fetish with the lad.

It was a single bedroom, so Aidan got the couch, which was spotless and quite enormous. There were blankets stacked on an end cushion. He checked the refrigerator, natch, and it was chock full of goodies. A perk of being a cook at the pub, he supposed. There was beer but no liquor. He checked the cupboards and found a bottle of Jameson, of which he availed himself forthwith and generously. He was partial to clear liquors, vodka the best, because it was essentially alcohol and water.

He watched a little TV while waiting for Liam's shift to end, and a little after 1 a.m., Liam arrived. He wasted little time in a welcome greeting. He closed the door and Aidan muted the TV.

"Where's the guy whose bike you stole? You know—the one you coldcocked at the pub?" Liam wanted answers *now*.

Aidan stood. "I'll tell you. But I'll tell you outside. Come with me," he said and headed toward the door. Liam blocked him.

"Why outside?"

"Humor me, brother."

Liam stepped aside and the brothers took the stairs and were soon in front of the apartment building.

"So start talking." Liam said.

"Watch this." And in two seconds Aidan was down at the end of the block, at least 100 yards away from Liam. He shouted, waving in the streetlamp light. *"Liam! Over here!"* And in another quick zip, he reappeared at Liam's side.

Liam just stared. "What just happened?"

"Keep watching." Aidan stepped over to a car parked on the street. It was a large car, a Honda Accord, late model. Aidan squatted and put his arms around the rear tire, and then stood. He was still holding the tire, and the car was tilted comically. He maneuvered a single palm beneath that rear tire and hoisted the Honda even more precariously into the air, holding it suspended with his single outstretched arm, his hand palming the bottom of the tire.

Liam still had no reaction. He just stared at his brother. "What the fuck is going on, Aidan?"

Aidan gently put the car to rest on all four tires and stood toe-to-toe with Liam.

"Try to hit me," Aidan said.

He expected Liam to protest this, but he did not. He hauled off and aimed at Aidan's jaw. No connection. Aidan dodged the blow so quickly that Liam didn't see him do it. Liam tried a quick left jab to the belly. No connection. In frustration he hailed ten more frantic blows at his brother and all his fists could find was air. Liam had had enough.

"WHAT THE FUCK IS HAPPENING HERE!" he screamed in frustration.

Aidan smiled. "Now let's go back inside and I'll explain."

They trod the steps back up to 311, Liam as if in a trance. When they entered the flat Liam simply threw himself down in his big chair and stared at his brother, an unspoken cue to start explaining himself.

"I'm what people call a vampire."

Liam shook his head wearily. "Fuck all and bollocks."

Aidan felt his fuse shortening. "You want to know where that gobshite ape that I flattened last night is? His body is in my car's boot."

"What did you do? You…"

"I killed him. I sucked the blood out of him until he died, then kept sucking till I was full. Then I threw his body in the boot of my Toyota," he explained, somewhat hotly. "And I don't know what to do with his body. So if you have any good ideas, let me know."

Liam laughed, but not a funny laugh. "Anything else I should know?"

"Yes. I can't go out in the sun. In the daytime. I can't go out. Even if it's cloudy. So I don't know how I'm going to get to school, and I'd appreciate any ideas you have *there*, also."

"How did this happen to you?" Liam was getting his bearing.

"Fiona. That frickin' phony priest at the parish-"

"I never liked that prick. Father what-the-fuck. O'Doul. Kevin O'Doul."

"Well, your instincts are good. The priest is a vampire. Been alive for centuries. Seduced Fiona. Well… raped Fiona is more like it, then he made her into what she made me."

"She did it to you then. That wasn't very nice of her."

"No. It wasn't. Turns out she's a very selfish girl at heart. She wanted me to be 'her consort for eternity,' or some shite like that she said to me. As soon as I came to my senses I threw her out of the old house where she was staying with me." Aidan paused, looking troubled. "And I'm not sure she'll let me be."

"What do mean, 'came to your senses'?"

Aidan was weary. "I'll fill in the details later, all right? You have the general outline. I've held nothing back from you."

"Do you eat food?"

"No."

"You just…"

"I drink blood."

"Nothing else?"

"Booze. The clearer the better, but your Jameson works in a pinch. D'ya mind?"

For the first time that night Liam laughed and went to the kitchen to get drinks for two, still shaky from the revelations but still not even close to coming around to the truth of Aidan's claim.

The next evening, after the sun had safely set, Aidan and Liam drove to the drug dealer's flat. Aidan asked Liam to stay in the car while he went inside "to set things straight."

Aidan identified himself at the door as Liam's brother and flashed a ready wad of thousands of euros to give to the dealer for his troubles with Liam. The doorman/enforcer frisked Aidan and led him to the dealer's office, with the barrel of a pistol pressing into Aidan's spine.

After they were introduced, Aidan spun and ripped the windpipe out of the enforcer's throat before he could press the trigger, then turned and pounced upon the dealer himself, promptly draining him of some, but not all, of his blood. (He had fed last night and was only 'topping off the tank' with this fellow.) Both men lay in a heap on the floor, the dealer gasping for breath as his neck still pumped out his lifeblood through two tiny holes. Aidan took out his own wallet and removed six €500 notes and a €100 note, crumbled them in his hand, and stuffed the wad of cash into the open mouth of the drug dealer.

"We pay our debts," Aidan said, "and now we're square." He thought, *you're the real blood-sucker.*

23

Fiona wept bloody tears on her way to Dublin after being thrown out, almost literally, of Aidan's family home, and by her true love himself. The clock in the dash said 10:00 in the p.m. and she would soon be at the city limits.

She had money, she had a car, and she had many clothes and accessories for her new life in the city, where she hoped she would never be found by anyone but her heart's desire, her dear Aidan Bell. She would go back to his old home soon and try to make peace with him. In a few days, she decided, after she gets settled in. He'll have snapped out of it by then!

She booked herself into the Conrad Dublin. She took a King Premier Room with a balcony. Very nice! She had never stayed in a hotel room in her life before 'Father' O'Doul took her to London. She so fell in love with the idea, and liked the King Premier in Dublin so much, she just might forgo the house idea until things become clear. Surely Aidan will want to share a home with her here in Dublin? Once he comes around?

But no. She took the words of her sire to heart, to be more frugal, and decided instead to rent a house here in Dublin until she reunited with her true love, and only stayed at the hotel for three glorious nights. She found a house to let in the East Wall section. A little shabby, but it was temporary. And the new feeding grounds were a target-rich environment.

After the sixth night of solitary living (and two near-disastrous feedings—she really needs to address this issue in her new environs without delay) Fiona decided to drive back to Aidan's home and try to make contact. She left at dark and had a comfortable ride.

Of course, Aidan wasn't there. The house was empty. Was he out feeding? No way to tell and nothing to do but wait! She broke in easily and watched some telly, which Aidan had not yet disconnected. She fell asleep at dawn and slept for hours. She woke about noon and became very upset. Could he have left the village? How could she be sure? She went into his bedroom and checked his closets and drawers. *All were empty!* He was gone!

She went back to the living room and sat, brooding frantically. She calmed gradually and her logical facility returned, such as it does to a woman like Fiona. She decided to call Aidan, though she avoided doing that all this time because she reasoned that it was a bad way to handle this situation. But she had no choice. She rang him up, but alas, his phone number no longer worked. The bastard must have gotten a new number. Then it occurred to her. Liam!

She started to call him and stopped before it connected. She could track him instead! She downloaded one of many illegal but appropriate apps for the job, installed it and entered Liam's number. He was in Dublin! She mapped the address and saw it was a pub called *The Vessel*. She would head there at dusk, but that was many agonizing hours away! She tried to sleep but had little luck, skipping on the surface of refreshing slumber but never entering therein, troubled for hours with evil dreams, tossing and turning in her anguish.

As soon as she could stand it, she left the house and started her drive back to Dublin. Her skin felt scalded, and she realized she had left the house too soon. She drove through the lessening discomfort, arriving at Dublin about 9 p.m. She drove straight to the pub.

She entered, noted a small crowd, sat, and told the skinny server girl she wanted a glass of gin on the rocks. When the young woman (it was Ronnie) returned with her drink she inquired after Liam.

"O, Liam? Sure. He's in the kitchen. Shall I tell him he has a visitor, then?"

"Yes, please." Fiona vowed to be on her best behavior.

Liam was all smiles when he left the kitchen, which quickly disappeared when he saw who his visitor was. He slowed his pace and cautiously took a chair across from a beaming Fiona.

"Liam," she piped with that lovely musical voice, offering her hand. "It's so good to see you."

He stared for a moment. "He told me," he said flatly, ignoring her hand. She pulled it back with a sniff.

"Is Aidan here too, then?" she asked, less sweetly.

"I haven't see Aidan. He called me and told me what he thought I needed to know. He refused to tell me where he was because he didn't want me to be able to tell anyone else," he lied. "So no. He isn't here and I don't know where he is."

Suddenly, Wee Dillon appeared beside Liam's chair. He smiled broadly, waiting for Liam to introduce him.

"Uh… Dillon, this is Fiona. Fiona, this is Dillon. He owns the place."

She extended her hand and Dillon gave it a squeeze. "A pleasure to meet you, Dillon."

Dillon was too bewitched to move, nodding stupidly and he may have mumbled something. Though her stunning beauty was lost on Liam, it was not lost on anyone else at the pub. Even the women couldn't stop looking.

Sensing the obvious, Liam looked up at Dillon and said, "I'll be back in the kitchen in two shakes."

"O! Good. Take a minute, though." He looked to Fiona. "And a pleasure to meet you. You'll come back often, we hope."

They sat for a moment in silence and Fiona took a gulp of her gin.

"You look well, Liam," she said with a smile, fishing for a complement.

"You look different," he said. "I liked you better before. When you were human. And not so selfish."

She tuned angry and her eyes caught fire. "I don't believe you don't know where your brother is!" she seethed. "I have something for him. I need to give it to him!"

Liam stood and glared at her. "You've given him enough. He didn't tell me where he was, 'for my own protection,' he said. Now I know why. Because of you. That's how he is. He thinks of other people no matter how it might hurt. Let him alone. And me. And don't let the door smack you in the arse on the way out."

She was so furious that it took all her effort to pretend otherwise. She finished her gin in a single long gulp, and when she put her glass down she called little Ronnie over—and ordered another. She'd be damned if she would be ordered about by the likes of Liam Bell. And it would be a lucky door that would smack *this* arse. The thought made her smile as the gin did its work.

As soon as Liam hit the kitchen he called Aidan.

"She's here," he said.

"Fiona?"

"No, Margaret Thatcher."

"Fuck all. How did she find you? I gotta get out. What did you tell her?"

"That you didn't tell me where you are for my own protection."

"Good. I'm out of your flat, brother. As of five minutes from now. Can I leave most of my stuff here?"

"Sure. No worries."

"I'll stay in touch."

Short and sweet. In five minutes Aidan was on his bike, his saddle bags brimming with the few necessities, headed to a nearby motel for the night and most of tomorrow. Or a week. Or who the hell knows!

Aidan operated out of his motel hideaway for two months. He had avoided Fiona, who was becoming reckless and frustrated in her attempts to locate Aidan.

Hunting and feeding became a treacherous business for both of them. Between himself and Fiona, investigators into the skyrocketing murders and missing person reports were bound to find their mark.

At last Aidan decided to leave the land of his birth and fly to a new life in the States. He wept at his resolve to leave his homeland and hoped that, unbidden, his brother might follow him. The thought shamed him, but even he had no idea of the devotion he sparked in his little brother since they were babies.

24

Fiona has just made two important purchases from her luxury hotel room in Ann Arbor. One is a laptop computer. She loves surfing the web to shop. Her second purchase is more unusual. O'Doul's threat to her at the airport is something she cannot shake off. It's the only thing in her life that frightens her. So, browsing for imaginative solutions to her unique problem, she saw rave reviews about something called an *XM42 Flamethrower Lite*.

She wanted one *now*, not *soon*, so she checked with gun stores in the Ann Arbor region until she found a vendor who would not only sell her one but show her how to use it after he closes up shop. She just bought it this evening, received her training and is quite thrilled.

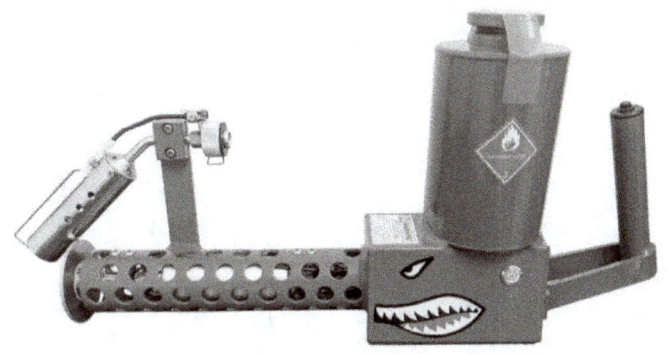

Fiona's XM42 Flamethrower Lite

Now she has a weapon against O'Doul, should he ever decide that Fiona has become "unworthy" of what he had "given" her.

Let him come, she thinks. *For he will come. And imagine that! In America you can buy a flame thrower! In a shop, even on the internet!* She laughs to herself. *Is this a great country or what!*

She even had a choice of colors and, natch, chose a nice bloody red.

25

Fiona had found Liam in Dublin, and now she finds him again in Ann Arbor.

It's a Sunday night and Liam is home enjoying many beers, marijuana cigarettes, novel American munchies and watching trash TV. Liam could not convince either of his two work colleagues to drop by for a snuggle. Seems more and more they have "something else planned. Sorry!" Aidan is out for a feed. All bets are off as to when he'll be back.

The doorbell rings and he rises quickly to answer, hoping one of the ladies has changed her mind.

It is Fiona.

"Hello," she says sweetly. "Shall we keep it civil?"

Liam is stunned to see her. His clouded mind races to no good result. "Of course. Civil."

"Lovely home," she said peeking inside. "But not yours, I'm guessing." She smiles. "Is Aidan home?"

"He's not."

She puts on a more stern face. "Civil, Liam, means asking me in."

He mumbles something in useless protest as Fiona slips past him.

"You always lie to me, Liam," she says, pacing through the house, checking rooms. "I'm afraid I can't take your word for these things. You're standing between Aidan and myself. You're in the way."

She even checks the basement. In that slender slice of time Liam calls Aidan, who answers immediately.

"She's here," he whispers, knowing that Fiona's hearing puts a bat's to shame. He disconnects immediately and remains standing in the middle of the living room.

Satisfied that there is no Aidan to be found, Fiona returns to the living room and stands in front of Liam.

"Just tell me where he is," she says in a weary voice.

"I don't know where he is because he's out feeding, as he calls it. I'm sure you know what that's all about."

"Where does he feed?"

"Anywhere from Jackson to Detroit, Flint to Toledo. Depends on his mood and recent pattern. Sound familiar?"

She considers all this. She sits at the end of one of the big couches. "I'll wait, if you don't mind."

"What if I *do* mind?" Liam asks.

Fiona simply offers a cold stare.

"I'm going to bed," Liam says and turns from her.

"*Wait!*" Fiona cries. Liam turns back. "If you're going to bed, give me your phone."

Reluctantly, he surrenders it, realizes his mistake, and heads to his room.

"*Wait!*" she repeats, and Liam stops. He turns and in despair sees that she is checking his call log.

"Liam, you bastard." She looks up and flings the phone to the floor. "You called him. When I was in the basement." She is growing angry and Liam is growing anxious. He steps back. She sighs. "I'm at the very end of my rope with you, Liam." She stands. "Be very careful from now on. At this point you're only alive because you're Aidan's brother."

She storms from the house and zooms away in her big Jaguar.

Liam hopes his phone isn't broken. He picks it up and pokes Aidan's speed dial. It connects.

"Liam?" Aidan answers.

"Yeah. Listen. She's gone. She knew I called you and she left."

"Did she hurt you?"

"No. But she was considering it."

"Okay. I won't be home tonight. I gotta think."

"Think for both of us, please."

"I'll stay in touch. And Liam."

"Aye."

"Turn location services off in that phone. She knows where we live, she doesn't need to know where you are, especially if you decide to lie low for a while. Which might be a good idea."

"Will do, brother. But I'll not abandon you."

26

Aidan went far afield for this latest meal, a motorcycle bar in Warren, a large, dense suburb of Detroit. All six men present rode Harley-Davidson hogs and they objected to Aidan's "Eurotrash" BMW in the same lot, contaminating their treasures, insisting that Aidan find another place to drink.

Aidan objected to their objection in less-than-respectful terms and was rushed at once by all six hairy and menacingly attired gentlemen. Aidan nimbly beat the six of them unconscious, paying not enough attention to the bartender who pulled a sawed-off shotgun from under the bar. His first shot went wide, and he never got a chance to fire a second.

Aidan has seven choices now and decides on the bartender because he seemed sober, and after all, just tried to kill him.

He likes to be high on alcohol, but through his own efforts rather than through the blood of another, and so he decides to head back to Ann Arbor and tour the pubs, rather, the 'bars,' on Main Street. Aidan has long held that 'drinking' rhymes with 'thinking' for a good reason.

Ruddy-faced with his recent meal and in peak possession of his powers, Aidan parks the big Beemer on the street and enthusiastically starts his tour of the surplus of overpriced bars and restaurants of downtown Ann Arbor.

After a couple hours of this Aidan is very drunk but disheartened that what he thought was going to be a fun discovery of the local watering holes is turning out to be a most sterile experience. He longs for the pubs of his home—the closeness, the families with their kids, the singing, the real music. Here the drinks are small, the people cocoon to themselves, and sonic horrors are piped in at oppressive volume levels. It all seems more about a trendy 'ambience' than about getting together with mates.

But more urgently, his mind is clouded with the subject of How to Confront Fiona. Specifically, he knows how she feeds, and he feels he needs to protect the children of the city, for he knows Fiona will feast upon them exclusively if given half a chance. She should not have come. Not to his city, not to befoul and desecrate his hometown.

Just thinking about this brings Aidan back to his days as a newborn, snatching babes from playpens two at a time. How many lives did he destroy? How many families? How many mums with broken hearts forever? Always more maudlin than usual when he's drunk, Aidan begins to weep at the flood of awful memories and flees the glitzy lounge he's long had enough of after a single drink.

Disgusted and blind drunk, he stumbles into a dive on the edge of downtown and decides to end his grand tour, settle in for a nightcap and then go home. Drinking helps you forget, right? *Right?*

He orders a vodka on the rocks. The bartender takes a good long look at Aidan, deciding whether he is too drunk to serve, but Aidan fixes him with a stare that compels him to pour the drink and bugger the fuck off. Once he's served, Aidan trudges off to the far table in the back, drink in one hand and stack of bar napkins in the other. Sitting there he weeps even harder, filling napkin after napkin with his scarlet tears.

An old man at the bar, the only other customer, can't seem to take his eyes off Aidan. Eventually he approaches Aidan and asks to join him. The old fellow gets a jolt looking at all the bloody napkins and the red streaks on Aidan's face.

"Allergies," he says.

"Right," says the old-timer. "Can I sit anyway?"

"Fuck all, why not," he slurs. "You're the only friendly face of the evening."

"You sound Irish."

"Aye. I'm trying to be an American, but I hate your bars."

"This, my Irish friend, can be a very bad town to find a nice friendly place such as the pubs to which you are accustomed."

"You like it here?"

"No students. No goddam TVs on the wall. A little rundown so no yuppies. It's cheap. They let me alone. Suits me." They laugh. "You know… it's not my custom to trouble anyone with my company, but a man sitting near me by himself crying bloody tears? Maybe I can help you sort things out. Can't hurt, eh?"

"Can't help. I'm irredeemable."

"No one's irredeemable."

"First of all, you don't understand; second, no God-talk please."

"Who said anything about God?"

"You and your redemption."

"'Irredeemable'—your word; not mine."

Aidan looks up at the old man, having to close one eye to stop the double-vision, and drops his head.

"Fuck all…"

"What did you do? That's so bad?"

Aidan tries to restrain himself but fails and bursts out crying, head down and shoulders shaking. This lasts a good minute. He lifts his head and stares hard at the old-timer.

"Okay mate, you asked for it," he whispers. "This'll send you running for the hills—*I murdered and ate children.* That's right. *Babies.* And their mums. And various and sundry other innocents, but it's the babies…" And here comes another volley of bloody tears, his head buried on the table in his arms.

Eventually he sits up and tries to wipe the mess off his face. "You still here?" He asks the old man, genuinely surprised.

"Is this something you still indulge in?" the man asked, calmly.

Aidan looks at him in wonder. "No. No it's not. A soon as I came to my senses I vowed never again!"

"Came to your senses? What do you mean?"

"I wasn't in my right mind." The tears are gone. Aidan just wants to talk. "You see… someone did something to me unasked. It took away my will. I had no choice in my actions."

"Are you certain?"

"Actually, yes. I am. I didn't used to be, but I am now! But it didn't take away my *memory.* Imagine living with that! I am *damned,* don't you see? And I've been transformed! *My soul has been taken from me!*"

"So, fight for its return."

Aidan is silent. He looks up at the old fellow. "What did you say?"

"I said, fight for its return."

Aidan considers this.

The old man goes on. "You never hurt the children as an act of will. That right?"

"I had no more choice than you do to breathe."

They sit for a moment in silence.

"Your sorrow," the old man says, "is the most authentic and passionate I've ever seen in a man. The only forgiveness needed here, or even possible, is that you stop wallowing in guilt you haven't earned."

He reaches out and seizes Aidan by his forelock to assure his attention and slaps him hard across the face. Aidan is too shocked to react. He sits, wide-eyed at the audacity of the old man, but he sits respectfully and attentive.

"Stop wallowing in guilt you haven't earned! It serves no good, no purpose. It's *unmanly.* Stop it! Let it go!" He pauses to let it sink in. "But you want to atone. That *is* manly. As far as compensation goes, you can only pay it forward. Keep vigilant. The time to redeem yourself may come upon you with slow clarity, or all of a sudden, like a thief in the night, but come it shall. Will you be ready?"

"I… I will."

"Will you be ready?"

"Yes."

"A final word, then."

"Jaysus. What?" He pulls his head back, expecting another wallop.

"Have faith in what shall unfold. Without faith, you are truly… well, we are *all* of us—truly *fucked. That's* what being damned is truly about." The old man sighs and shakes his head. "See, if you believe your soul is truly lost, then truly it is. It's all up to you."

They sit in silence for a few minutes, Aidan lost in thought, halfheartedly nursing his drink.

Finally, the old fellow stands, looking down on the inebriated mess that is Aidan Bell. Aidan struggles to get on his feet and extends his hand. "Thanks for sitting with me. It was... generous of you."

The man takes Aidan's hand in both of his own and presses it. He turns and heads out of the bar. Aidan sits back down with a heavy sigh and bolts back what is now tepid vodka and water. He is suddenly very tired. He puts his head down on his arms and rests. The old man has rocked his world.

The bartender is next to him and pokes him.

"No naps here, pal. Time to move on, eh?"

"Yeah. Okay." Aidan pushes himself up unsteadily. "What was the name of that old gentleman?"

"What old gentleman," the bartender asked, annoyed.

"Jesus—the fellow I was sitting here with for the last half hour!"

"Buddy, you been sitting there crying like a woman and talking to yourself like a fucking lunatic and bloodying up all my goddam napkins. That'll be a joy to clean up." He heads back behind the bar. "Come on. Time to go. Sell crazy somewhere else."

Aidan can't believe this! "There!" he points. "He was sitting *right there*. At the bar."

"You've been the only one here for the last hour. Now *please*, go home. Or just somewhere else. I can't serve you anymore. You've had enough."

Aidan has never been so drunk in his life and certainly never so sitting on a motorcycle. With all his concentration and with one eye closed, he putters down Huron to Jackson Road to the Weber's hotel at which he stayed when he first arrived, and requests the same room, which is available. He stumbles through his door and throws himself on his bed. When he wakes he'll have no idea where he is or how he got there.

He won't know until evening when he ventures out, that his bike has been stolen because he failed to secure it. He actually failed to turn it *off*. He just blundered off of it, fell on his ass, stood back up with great effort and staggered into the hotel.

The next morning he calls in sick to the college. He still has no idea how to outfit his Subaru to protect him from the sun. He might have to buy another bike, but that is just postponing the problem.

27

It takes Fiona three days to leave the Holiday Inn and find a house to rent in Ann Arbor. It is furnished garishly (even she thinks so, so imagine!) bigger than she requires, on a half-acre, near town, with a huge two-car garage. The house is across from an elementary school. All the activity there takes place during sunlight hours, leaving Fiona longing in vain for a blast of that sweet innocent blood. So near, yet so far away...

Fiona's Fateful House

It's right after sunset now and a little uncomfortable but she needs to feed. She backs her big Jaguar out of the garage and decides to enter the school drive and circle the grounds. Why not? Around back in the lot she sees four cars, and moms and children scattered about near the back entrance of the school. She stops and watches, braking hard in her mind against her bloodlust that might make her do something stupid if she isn't cautious.

She spies a minivan with writing on the side pulling up near the door and stopping. It's a large passenger van and the writing on the side reads, 'Ann Arbor Community Elementary.' Fiona wonders, *maybe an after-school program? This late?* She counts as the children enter the van. Eight in all. The doors close and the kids are zoomed away, a few of the moms still gaggling together, talking and laughing.

A plan takes place in that perfect perverted mind of hers. She wonders, *how often does that van come? Every evening?* She thinks of pursuing the van to see where it leads, but realizes that, as her plan is forming, it doesn't really matter where it's headed. *That's food for almost a month! Keep them locked in the van, fed and watered till I'm ready for one. Or two.* She needs to consider all this more carefully and not do anything rash or reckless.

Proud of her sense of maturity, she drives off to find sustenance. *Maybe a handsome college lad,* she thinks, *who needs a little lovin'!*

28

Liam, for his part, will not abandon his brother. They sit together, the evening after Aidan's colossal solo bacchanal. He's recovered fully, well, mostly, and recounts to himself over and again the events of that strange night.

"You're pretty quiet tonight," Liam says, offering his brother a vodka on the rocks. Aidan scrutinizes it with a wince, takes it and places it on the side table. Liam sits with his beer on the couch.

"It's Fiona."

"No shit!"

"Aye… you're shocked."

"What exactly?"

"I know I need to confront her as soon as I can. I don't know why I didn't consider this before. I hope I'm not already too late."

"Why?"

"Because… she gonna start in on the children. I can't let her d-"

"Jesus Christ! She's going to eat kids?! You sure?!"

"Aye. I know her, brother. If she hasn't already."

Liam drains his beer and stands. He goes to his brother. "Aidan. For christsake do what you have to do and do it quick. If you need me, tell me what to do and don't be afraid to use me. She doesn't scare me. I mean… she *does* scare the living bejesus out of me, but… but I'm not *afraid* of her. That make sense?"

Aidan smiles his appreciation.

"I'll be back tonight," Liam says. "Stay in touch."

Fiona doesn't know about Aidan's Subaru wagon (or Liam's Jeep). Now that the Beemer is gone it's how

Aidan will get around, and it's a much better vehicle to keep tabs on Fiona than that monster bike might have been. He decides to put a tail on her, and to start now. Trouble is, he doesn't know where she lives.

No way out of this but to call her. Ask to see her at her place because Liam is having his dream threesome tonight at his house, or something! Tell her something. No choice.

He pokes her number and she picks up.

"Aidan! It's you!" Such a sweet, lyrical voice.

"Hello, Fiona."

"Where are you, dearest?"

"I stepped outside the house. Liam is enjoying two waitresses at the same time in the living room and I was feeling a little... unnecessary. I'd be angry but it's a dream come true for the lad. Heh-heh."

"Do you want to come and see me?"

"Aye... aye I do, Fiona. We have much to discuss. It's been a long time."

"Come now! I miss you so. It's a house. Here's my address. Ready?... It's in town. 611 Lakes Street. Off Miller. Across from the school."

The school! Aidan thinks. *O Christ.*

"Are you still there, dear?" Fiona asks.

"Yes. Yes! I'll see you right away."

He disconnects and immediately has an idea. He calls Fiona back. She picks up and greets him.

"Fiona... remember when you came back home after you went off with that priest?"

"I do."

"And how you wouldn't see me straightaway. You had to wait for the right time?"

She sighs. "I remember."

"Well… it seems like such a big step. Deciding to come to you again. I need to do it when I'm ready. And I almost am!" he hurries to add. "In a day or two I'm guessing… but I have your number and I'll call, and if you still want to see me…"

"I'll always be there to see you, dear Aidan whom I've missed so much. This is terribly disappointing, but if it's what you need then-"

"It is! It is. But it won't be long. Until then."

"I love you, Aidan."

He hesitates, then spits the deceit out through clenched teeth: "I love you too, Fiona. Goodbye now."

He has her address.

Aidan hops in the Subaru and makes the drive to town, easily finding her house. He drives by slowly. Dark except for a light in what looks like the living room. He passes by, turns around, and parks three houses away. He shuts the car off and prepares himself for a sleepless night.

Sleepless and uneventful, for it would soon be dawn. Either she had fed earlier, or she needn't feed right now. He doesn't know her habits. And when she does leave the house, will it be to feed or to party? Or both? He'll know better soon.

The next evening as the sun had safely set, Aidan took up the same position he had taken the night before, keeping careful watch. He didn't have to wait long, for as soon as it was safe, Fiona's Jaguar backs out of the drive and onto the road. He starts the car and takes it out of park but stays put. It seems she's just driving across the street.

She takes a quick turn into the nearest entrance to the school lot and heads toward the back. Aidan stays put a few doors down from Fiona's house, car and lights off.

She travels around the school and comes out now through the second entrance which is behind him. He ducks down and she cruises past him. He peeks up and watches her pull back into her driveway and back toward her garage.

He waits a good minute before he starts up, pulls into the entrance she had just pulled out of and slowly drives toward the back of the school, tracing her path. He stops and notes an empty lot and a dark school entrance at the back. He completes the circuit driving along the side of the school and pulls out onto the street from the first entrance. He cruises around the block and repositions himself in the surveillance position.

What the hell was she looking for? He wonders. He resumes his sentry post and squirms around to get a bit more comfortable.

It shall be another long and uneventful night.

29

Liam had not lied when he told his brother that he had given up the opioid pills when they were still in Dublin. Here in Ann Arbor, a bottle of 30 Vicodin, for example, can go for several hundred dollars on the street. This is way out of Liam's reach, and he's not the type to rob gas stations to make some extra drug money.

What he hasn't told Aidan about, is his recent acquaintance with heroin. He keeps his 'tool kit' in his car. So far, his job has made the purchases viable, and he uses it sparingly enough that it hasn't interfered with his duties at work. Aidan is back to sleeping days and hunting nights, so it's easy to work around his presence. The problem with the new user's occasional indulgence in heroin is that this condition almost never stays on that low plateau. Combine this with Liam's addictive personality and it's hard not to sense a pending catastrophe.

But there is a moderating influence that is stronger than all these discouraging factors, and that is Liam's devotion to his brother. He needs to stay sharp, and if anything, his drug use is less now than had been in the past two weeks.

Liam asked Aidan if he knew where Fiona lived. He said he did not. Liam did not believe his brother. Last night he followed Aidan when he left the house after dusk "to go see Sylvia." Liam smelled a deception. Aidan and Sylvia are experiencing some trouble in paradise lately and Liam overheard that she wants to "take a break."

Liam put a tail on Aidan last night, parked down the block and also noted Fiona come out of her house to case the schoolyard. He knows now where Fiona lives.

His guess is that Aidan was further trying to protect him by keeping this from him.

He will follow Aidan again tonight. Liam is terrified of Fiona's obsession with the elementary school.

Doubly so is Aidan.

30

This time Aidan parks in the back lot of the school, with Fiona's house in his line of sight across the street. He knows that Fiona is waiting for something to happen here, behind the school.

Liam had again left before Aidan while the sun was still setting in order to get positioned far enough that Aidan would not note Liam's presence upon his arrival. He parked where Aidan would not pass him on his way to Fiona's, but near enough to keep a cold eye on her should she emerge. But when he sees Aidan pull into the school drive and not come out, Liam ventures closer, parking now just a few doors down from Fiona's house.

Both brothers note the activity of a few cars going in and out of the drives. Aidan sees moms and schoolkids talking and playing outside near the rear entrance of the school, obviously waiting for something.

At the stroke of dark Fiona's Jaguar appears from her garage and she turns into the school lot. She tools around back, slows down, and continues out the far exit and back up her driveway and into the garage. This befuddles the brothers, but they stay put.

After a few minutes, a white passenger van pulls in and drives behind the school. Aidan watches as the door opens and eight excited boys and girls spring on board waving bye to their moms. The driver, a slim older women, has a clipboard in her hand and is scribbling something, occasionally shouting back to the kids. She has not yet closed the door.

Both brothers now note that Fiona has emerged from her house, but only Liam can see her walking to the far exit of the school grounds instead of the nearest one. She stops at the exit and does not proceed. She stands there, as if she is waiting for something.

Aidan watches the van full of children pull away from the school's rear entranceway, starts his car, and follows it out of the lot at a distance. Both brothers now see the van slow down as it approaches Fiona at the foot of the exit, who appears to be flagging the van to a stop. The van driver does stop and opens the door to see what Fiona wants. She slides in, the door closes and there is a brief commotion visible, but the details aren't clear. Soon the van turns out of the lot. What *is* clear—*is that Fiona is now driving it.*

Both brothers are unprepared for this development and follow the van at a distance. Aidan, who is in front of Liam, notes Liam's presence for the first time. He tells his phone to call Liam on speakerphone and Liam answers.

"What are we gonna do?!" Liam yells.

"Don't tailgate me, Liam. I'm going to drop back. Leave some space. We'll follow. I don't want her to make us."

"Don't hang up!" Liam cries. *"Stay on the line."*

"Okay. Calm down."

Fiona turns down a dirt road, and both Aidan and Liam smartly ignore the turn, driving straight on. They turn around and slowly creep back down the street until the van comes into view for Aidan, Liam right behind him in his Jeep. Aidan sees that Fiona has stopped the van about 200 yards down the dirt road.

"I can see her, Liam."

"What do we do?"

"I guess we wait."

"And hope she's not killing kids while we just sit here on our dead arses?!"

"I don't think so. I think she's just waiting till the moms clear out from the school."

"You do? Why?"

"I think she wants *all* the kids. Not just a quick meal."

"Really?"

"Aye." Aidan says, then adds. "It's what I would do. If I were her."

Five minutes pass, the slowest five minutes of the brothers' lives. Finally the van starts up, the headlights flick on and Fiona is turning the van around in a driveway. Aidan hits the gas.

"Liam! Follow me down the street and park well behind me. Understand?"

"Yes. I got it."

"And keep your head down."

"Will do."

"Car and lights off."

"Got that. Not stupid."

The brothers are in place and Aidan spies Fiona turning in their direction. She zips past both brothers and turns toward her home at the next corner. The men start their cars and follow cautiously.

Aidan was right. Fiona turns into her driveway and pulls the big van into the garage. The door closes.

Aidan has no choice but to act, making it up as he goes along. Via the phone he orders Liam to stay in his car.

"Did you hear me, Liam?"

No response.

"Liam, goddammit. *Stay in your fucking car. You are not up to this.*"

No response.

"Shit!"

131

Liam pulls up to Fiona's house and runs up to her door. He rings the bell. And waits.

And rings again.

And waits.

He thinks of the kids on the bus and braces himself to blast down the door.

But at the moment of his resolve the door unlocks and opens, and there stands Fiona, not with a dazzling smile for her prodigal lover, come to her at last, but with a nervous frown.

"Ah… Aidan. Umm…"

Cautiously. "Hello, Fiona."

"Did you see me drive in?"

"No, no I didn't. I got here this second. Did you just get home?"

At that Fiona relaxes and gives him that dazzling smile.

"Come in, my love. At last."

Aidan enters and Fiona closes the door. She turns and drapes her arms about Aidan's neck… and they kiss. Deeply and passionately. Aidan almost forgets why he's here.

They separate and Fiona offers him a drink.

"Vodka please? Maybe some ice?"

"Be right back, love," she whispers and vanishes into the kitchen, retuning in moments with two identical drinks. She bids Aidan sit and get comfy and hands him his drink. He gulps down half and places the glass on a side table. Fiona sits across from him.

"So Aidan, have you come back to me? I've thought of nothing else."

Aidan skootches forward in his chair and leans toward Fiona, elbows on his knees, eyes down.

"Well… I think first we need to talk."

She darkens. "About what?"

Aidan is silent, searching for words.

"It's not that complicated, Aidan. Do you love me?"

He looks up. "Fiona… we can discuss love, but there is something more urgent."

She is visibly annoyed.

"What is so urgent, then?"

"Before we sort out our own situation… I need you to release the children."

She leaps to her feet and screams at Aidan.

"YOU DECEITFUL BASTARD!"

"Fiona, just-"

"You hate me," she seethes. *"You still hate me."* She begins pacing the room, anger seeping from her pores into the air. Aidan could smell it.

"I will not be told by you, or anyone else, how and on what I may FEED! This is *my business!* You ungrateful *bastard.* I gave you eternal life! And you return that gift with hate and treachery! *And sneak into my house!"*

Aidan is on his guard. She could spring at him at any moment. He is stronger, but she is much more clever.

"Fiona, listen to me, please. Just listen."

She stops pacing and sits, her jaw is tight, and her teeth are gritted. But the eyes—her eyes are an emblem of raw animal hate.

"Say your piece."

"I will. Thanks. Now, if-"

"Wait," she says. "I need another drink. Do you want another?"

"No." He looks at his half-filled glass. "I'm fine."

Fiona heads toward the kitchen and Aidan listens for the familiar tinkle of glass and the pouring of the bottle but he senses none of that. *And she has been gone almost a minute,* he thinks. *Where the hell-?* He looks and notes that she hadn't touched her drink.

Fiona reappears, holding not a glass, but a device of some kind. The room floods with the odor of gasoline.

"What… what is that thing?" Aidan whispers.

She grins a feral grin. "It's a flame-thrower."

Aidan springs up, but Fiona warns him.

"One more move. If I even *sense* that you are about to move—and isn't that a wonderful attribute we share?— I will end you forever."

Aidan is astonished. "A flame-thrower?"

"I got it to protect me from the good Father O'Doul who *raped* me then threated my existence. I will suffer that from *no one!* I never thought I would turn it on you. But *you* are the greater threat."

"Fiona, put that down and let's talk."

"That meat out there in the van is *mine!*" she rages. "I obtained it through my wiles. It's what I am! It's what I do! It's what *we* do."

"No!' Aidan objects. "Not *we.*"

"And what will happen to me if I do as you wish? Have you considered that? There is a dead woman in the van. There are eight terrified wee brats that will tell the same story to the guards, I mean, the police. I *like* my life in the States. I like my house. And I will not permit you to endanger me in *any way.* You ungrateful *bastard!*"

"I *am* ungrateful. You took my soul from me. You made me into a monster."

Fiona laughs but is not distracted.

"I gave you immortality! The greatest gift imaginable!"

Now it's Aidan who laughs.

"You don't see it, do you? This is how we, we the soulless, this is how all of us *end.* Accident maybe, but more likely violence. It may take centuries, but when it comes we are *completely ended.* But the ones you call mortal? Those who are ensouled are the *true* immortals. They are the ones who move from life to life forever. *We all had it backwards!* It is *they* who are the true immortals, not us. It is *we* who *truly die."*

The room crackled with it. Aidan senses it. There is nothing he can do. His fate is sealed at this very moment. Fiona's brain has sent the message to her trigger-finger.

The front door bursts open and there appears a grim but terrified Liam.

Here is what Fiona and Aidan see: Without moving her head, Fiona's eye catches the door swing open and she sees Liam, deciding to ignore him and concentrate on Aidan. In that distracted millisecond of her calculation, Aidan springs upon her but not before Fiona senses this, presses the trigger and Aidan is soaked with a fiery blast of napalm to the front of his body. His momentum carries him to crash into Fiona, and the pair rocket against the wall, Fiona losing control of the weapon and it falls to the floor. Fiona's clothing has caught fire from the flaming Aidan, who is now on top of her.

Here is what Liam sees:

He bursts through the door and senses a blur and a flash of fire that resolves with two bodies burning on the floor, Aidan is lit like a torch and Fiona is beneath him. The flamethrower is at Liam's feet. Liam snatches it up.

Fiona flings Aidan's burning body off of her where it smashes into the opposite wall and lands in a deranged heap, burning and smoldering. She panics at the flames engulfing her clothing and before she can stand up, Liam presses the button on the weapon and Fiona is literally hosed with fire. She screams and falls back to the floor, writhing in agony. The entire half of the living room is now on fire.

Liam rushes to his brother. He is partly burnt to a crisp, but he is still alive.

"Aidan! O my God! Brother!" Liam cries, kneeling at his side.

"The children…" Aidan murmurs almost inaudibly. "Free the kids… in the garage."

"I'm getting you out of here first!" Liam cries.

"No!" Aidan is seized with a spasm of agony. "No. I'm done. The house… is on fire. Save… save the kids."

Liam stands and looks at his brother and as he comes to his senses he knows that Aidan is right. There is not a patch of skin on the front of his brother that is not charred black or else a scarlet oozing blister.

"I'll be back!" Liam cries, but in his heart knows he has seen the last of his dear Aidan.

The fire is spreading wildly, and Liam rushes out of the room to find an entrance to the garage. He locates it, opens the door and there is the white van parked next to Fiona's Jag. There are many children inside, all of them crying, banging upon the windows, and screaming hysterically.

The doors are locked! Fiona has the keys but the housefire has spread so fast that smoke is coming into the garage. He dares not reenter the house. Liam looks about him and finds not a single implement of any kind to break the glass of the van. He hits the button to open the garage doors and runs to his car. He retrieves the jack handle from the Jeep's spare tire compartment and rushes back.

Liam pounds on the driver side glass with the jack handle and the window finally shatters into smithereens of little cubes of safety glass. He reaches in and unlocks the door. The screams of the children are so dreadful! They rush to the open door and fall all over one another in their escape, but no one is hurt. They scamper to the front of the house and watch in morbid fascination as the house goes up in flames, lighting up the evening. Liam finds the body of the van driver and tugs her loose from behind the front seat and out of the van. A neighbor helps Liam drag the body to the front yard. Another neighbor brings a blanket to cover her.

There are neighbors and gawkers everywhere, the more useful ones calming and caring for the children. Liam calls 911 in case no one else has. Fire and rescue, he is told, are in route. He hears the sirens.

31

Aidan is truly alone. His agony is unmatched by anything in his memory. He lay there, waiting and praying for his annihilation to come at last.

Even through the crushing anguish Aidan finds, as his life ebbs away, a quiet refuge at his center to reflect. He considers his life, his few loves, his trials and errors and now it is as if a curtain is descending, and though the searing flames have taken his eyes, he clearly sees…

"Ma!" he croaks in a whisper voice. *"Ma! It's you!"*

He raises his arm a bit and shudders in anguish. *"I'll take your hand, ma! I'll come along.*

Are you taking me home?

O ma! It hurts so bad…"

EPILOGUE

Liam is back in Ireland, but not back to work. When he arrived two months ago he was embraced by Dillon and the whole crew at *The Vessel*, all so glad that he was back safely home.

Aidan has a will, and the sole beneficiary is Liam. This money Liam will not refuse because it is Aidan's, not his father's. But the situation is not yet settled, and he is still waiting for the money. Liam is now incredibly wealthy but has to steal to eat.

He started work immediately but by the 10th day Dillon told him that he was finished. He was caught stealing money from a customer's purse while she was in the jacks. That was actually the last straw as his performance and punctuality had become increasingly unreliable.

Only Veronica had taken his part, making excuses for him because of the trauma he suffered in the States and, of course, the loss of his brother. Liam is strung out so badly on heroin that his few friends fear for his life.

This evening, it's Sunday, Ronnie has dropped by to check on Liam. He is a mess and so is his flat. She does the few dishes that have been sitting for days and tries to straighten up so that one can at least walk around the flat without stepping on clothes or bottles or worse.

She finishes tidying up and sits next to a very smelly Liam on the couch. He's in a haze. He looks at little Ronnie and bursts into tears. She tries to comfort him, but he will have none of it. He pushes her away. She thinks he's revolted by her, but Liam knows it's shame, pure and simple.

"I gotta go, Liam. It's late," she says. "Unless..."

Liam looks at her as if he just noticed her in his flat.

"Aye. Okay. Go on then," he mutters. She takes his hand in her own. He lets her.

"Come back to us, Liam," she pleads. He pulls his hand away.

"Go on now," he whispers. "It's no use."

With a big sigh, Veronica takes her leave of the flat.

Ronnie finally gone, Liam grabs his works out of the table drawer, loads his spoon with triple the usual amount and begins the process of reducing the precious powder to a liquid. When he's done, he carefully attaches a fresh needle and loads up his fancy glass rig. He's made himself a 'hotshot.' When Liam mainlines this all his troubles will be over. He stares at the syringe.

He laughs bitterly, stands, and flings the loaded syringe at the far wall. He hears it shatter. He sits back down and weeps desperately. He has no more heroin. He has no more money.

There is a knock at the door. Then another.

"Goddamn it, Ronnie!" he shouts as he struggles to his feet. "What is it now!" It could only be her because no one else ever visits.

He tugs the door open and spies a gritty fellow clad in overalls and boots. He looks like a dock worker.

"Excuse me," the man says, "but are you Liam Bell?"

"Does he owe you any money?" Liam gruffs. The man snorts a little laugh.

"No. No. I'm... I'm Fiona's uncle. I'm Finn. Maybe she mentioned me. Belfast side of the family."

"We weren't friends," Liam says, staring at the fellow.

"Well, you see... I know she's dead. And it shames me that I didn't see her as much as I should have. And... anyway, may I come in for a moment?"

Liam looks up and down at the man and decides to let him in. He swings the door open.

"Sure. C'mon in. Brighten my night."

Liam resumes his seat and Finn sits across.

"Anyway, what can I do for you. Flynn."

"Finn," he corrected. "I want to know what happened to Fiona. She was such a lovely niece. And I miss her. And I know you were with her and your brother, Aidan, is it?"

"It was… it ain't no more."

"Yes. And I'm sorry. I can't imagine anything worse than what you must have gone through."

They sit in silence for a space.

"You want to know what happened? I'll tell you." He stands up. "Let's move to the kitchen table. I wanna roll some dope."

They adjourn to the table, and Liam talks while he rolls.

"Your niece was in love with my brother since… well, I never knew when she *wasn't* in love with my brother. He didn't return the feeling, but she could never believe that that was the case. He moved to America, she followed him, tracked him down like a goddam bloodhound," he stops and laughs to himself. "Heh heh… 'bloodhound.' Anyway… she found him, finally got it through her perfect thick head that Aidan would never love her, and she did what any nice normal girl would do—she tried to kill him."

"How?" Finn asks, almost reluctantly.

"She set him on fire." Liam runs his tongue along the edge of the rolling paper and gives the joint a squeeze and a roll. He holds it up in the air. "Ta-da!"

Finn has his elbows on the table and his face buried in the palms of his hands.

"Well… So anyway," Liam continues, "it all backfired on her, and they killed each *other*. I was a witness. I had some issues, and I was deported. And here I am. That answer your question?" he asks coldly.

Finn is weeping softly. "She was such a lovely girl," he sobs. "She died from a love ill-chosen." A single tear escapes his cheek and falls to the table.

A single ruby-colored tear.

Liam is frozen. 'Finn' looks up slowly and smiles at Liam.

"Well. Father O'Doul." Liam whispers.

He seizes Liam's wrist and holds tight.

"No. I was no more Father O'Doul then than I am Finn now. But no less. Finn is who I am at present."

Liam is speechless with dread.

"Now," Finn says, fixing Liam with a terrible glare. "Tell me what *really* happened."

Liam calms quickly and explains all, leaving out not a single detail. He senses his life is in danger and he is correct. When he finishes, Finn closes his eyes and they both sit in silence for many minutes.

"You killed Fiona," Finn says. "You are a remarkable young man."

Liam is silent. Terrified and mute.

"It took me three centuries to find a protégé," Finn whispers, "and it took her, what, two months? So impetuous! Such poor impulse control! Such a poor decision on *my* part. She should not have done such a thing to your brother and you were right to kill her. If you didn't, I would have. But this is my fault, and I'm sorry."

It takes a full minute till Finn snaps out of his reverie. He sits up straight and considers Liam.

"You live like a pig and you stink," he observes. "You are a drug addict?"

Liam sighs. "That's right."

"Heroin?"

Liam nods.

"Wonderful drug. Mine was opium. I took it for years in Turkey. Came as a young man to visit and stayed in the fog for years. I almost turned out as badly as you."

"Are you going to kill me?"

Finn laughs. "Yes, but how can you even care? See how you live." He waves a slow hand about the room. "What a worthless piece of trash you've become. Do you really care if it all ends now?"

"I dunno," Liam closes his eyes.

"Ah, but you know too *much*, Liam. About me, your brother, Fiona. How we live. I can't permit that."

Liam opens his eyes and glares at his tormentor.

"Well, then maybe you can go *fuck* yourself. I'm not afraid of you. I mean, I'm scared *shitless* of you, but I'm not *afraid* of you. You're a goddam monster and I'm not afraid of you!"

Finn laughs a deep belly-laugh and smiles. He reaches into the pocket of his overalls and takes out a small penknife, opens in, and places it on the table. He snatches Liam by the hair and pulls him forward. He tilts Liam's head and rests his chin in the crook of Liam's neck.

He whispers in Liam's ear. "You *are* a remarkable young man."

Finn opens his jaws, and his canine teeth extend to their full length and piercing keenness. He pauses.

"Have you ever been to London, lad?"

He doesn't wait for an answer.

⊂⊃

Ann Arbor, Michigan
During the Covid-19 hysteria lockdown
April to May 2020

About Gerald Brennan

I was born on September 2, 1953, in Jessup, PA. At age two I moved to Dearborn, MI, where I lived with my family until my late teens. The eldest of six children, I went to Catholic school, and when my brain started working at about age 15, I left the Church, my youthful mind appalled by its many dogmas. Nor did the priests and nuns wish to indulge my curious nature. When we had philosophical questions, the answer was usually along the lines of "Shut up." It was in high school that I began to write down the music in my head.

Wandering in the desert for many years, I drank heavily, experimented with drugs, and studied music, science and philosophy. Though I never had any formal music education, living in Ann Arbor put many wonderful resources at my disposal, including many fine Steinway grands sprinkled merrily throughout the University of Michigan campus back in the day when there didn't need to be a lock on every door. I became a good pianist in the following years, as well as composer. I had many musical adventures—breaking a Steinway grand playing Liszt at the University of Michigan music school, playing Liszt's American Steinway at the Smithsonian Museum in an impromptu recital that drew quite a wondrous crowd.

I became a National Public Radio affiliate producer with WUOM, WVGR and WFUM out of the U-M. I produced hundreds of weekly programs in my decade there—including *The Musical Theatre, New Music, New Releases, From the Monophonic Era, Music of Our World, Excursions* and *Nocturne.*

In 1980 I organized the Ann Arbor-based Sinewave Studios for the development and propagation of new art music. I produced about 20 concerts and conducted the North American premiere of Karlheinz Stockhausen's *Für kommende zeiten* at the Detroit Institute of Art.

My writing career started in 1984 when I wrote and self-published a booklet on starting a classical record collection. Borders Books agreed to carry it, and it finally made its way into the paws of a publisher. They asked me to expand it into a sure enough book and thus was born *Classical Records, Starting Your Collection*. After it was published, I took it to the Ann Arbor News and asked them if they needed a music reviewer. Turned out they did, and so, all while I had the radio gig, I was reviewing the best acts in the world that came through town.

Before all that I worked in record stores, including the famous Liberty Music. I also sold pianos, moved pianos, sold sheet music, managed U-M's record and sheet music store, and wrote for various national music journals.

In 1998, I was headhunted by a visionary fellow named Michael Erlewine, who decided that it would be a good idea to get hold of every album in the world and put every bit of information about it into a database. Eventually the idea included taking a photo of the album and doing sound samples. They started with a core of a few music geeks and began by going through their own collections. The company Erlewine founded was called *All Media Guide* (www.allmusic.com), which became the world's largest repository of product data and editorial information about music.

Erlewine asked me to assume the post of Director of Content of Classical Music at AMG, to create a department that would be devoted to classical music. I jumped at it, and in four years my amazing staff and I, along with scores of excellent writers, amassed the data, created the classical website, and produced the giant reference book, *AMG Guide to Classical Music,* which I edited and saw published in 2005. My mission was accomplished; my staff was a well-oiled machine and easily the best and happiest of all AMG's departments. Then 'investor fatigue' set in among the shareholders and AMG was appointed a slick new president who knew little about what we did or why but was hired to sell the company at a good price to whomever, and fast. He instinctively disliked me and my open resistance to his schemes and I was fired. I had no hard feelings. I had completed my mission, and it was time to go.

Now I write music and books, make recordings, and give the rare recital.

Books include this one, also *Prince of Pines*, a dystopian male-adventure novel set in Michigan's Upper Peninsula; *The Complete Short Stories;* the recent *The Angel Jophiel*, a fantasy novel about the classical music world and an angel sent to Earth to help rejuvenate the dying Arts, and *A Song of Blood and Ashes,* a vampire tale set in contemporary Ireland and Ann Arbor. Also, *Classical Music & Recordings–a primer,* and *Views & Reviews - Chronicles from the Twilight of the Golden Age of Classical Music*

Musically, I've to date got 90 songs published in three *SongBooks*, several chamber and orchestral pieces, piano works, a full-length Broadway-style musical called *Penelope*, choral works, and a large orchestral piece known as *Sinfonia Matrix,* which requires some 80-octillion years to be heard in its entirety. Therefore, performance versions are extracted depending upon available forces, duration required and occasion.

Available CDs include *Mythos* (piano pieces based upon Greek myth characters, recorded in recital and in-studio), *Five Fantasy Nocturnes for piano, Campfire—The Burning Psaltery* (a phantasmagorical piece for an innocent 12-string psaltery), *7 Solo Songs from 'Penelope,'* and several CDs from the *SongBooks* recorded in studio and at home, by me and various performers.

Also available on CD is the electronically-based Ambient Music Series, which includes *Ambient Counterpoint, Grand*

Starbells, Monochrome Frescos, The Singing Moon, and *Whisperings of Angels.*

All items detailed above are published by DreamStreet Press and available on Amazon or through DreamStreetPress.com.

Other Books by Gerald Brennan

Jophiel

Jophiel, Angel of the Beauty of the Divine Presence, incarnates in a mid-western town to a lovely woman and her outlaw husband in this tale set in near-future America.

Prince of Pines

Pure unapologetic dystopian male-adventure, intelligent and well-crafted, with plenty of guns and good women.

THE COMPLETE SHORT STORIES

Contemporary tales in many different genres.

SONG OF BLOOD & ASHES

An ancient Vampire finally creates a protégé after centuries of searching. Blinded by her beauty and innocence, his choice was unwise. She loves a 'mortal' who does not reciprocate her affection. Her depraved appetites provoke a most horrifying catastrophe.

Classical Music & Recordings

This book is intended as an introduction to the species of art music which we call Classical Music.

Views & Reviews

This book contains the original unedited versions of Gerald Brennan's previews, reviews, and interviews of the finest classical music soloists, ensembles, and orchestras in the world during what may well be looked back upon as the final flowering of Classical Music in the West.